A sudden cry ripped the heavy air. As Conan swung around, he caught a flicker of movement in the bushes at the junction of road and river. With a short bark of warning, Conan reined his steed, and an arrow meant for him flashed past his breast and, swift as a striking viper, buried itself in the neck of a young officer behind him. As the dying man slumped into the roiling water, Conan spurred his horse forward, bellowing orders.

Suddenly Fury reared and staggered beneath the impact of another arrow. With a shriek, the animal fell to its knees, hurling Conan from the saddle. The Cimmerian gulped a swirl of muddy water and struggled to his feet, coughing curses. Men howled war cries, screamed in fear and pain, and cursed the very gods above...

Chronological order of the CONAN series:

CONAN
CONAN OF CIMMERIA
CONAN THE FREEBOOTER
CONAN THE WANDERER
CONAN THE ADVENTURER
CONAN THE BUCCANEER
CONAN THE WARRIOR
CONAN THE USURPER
CONAN THE CONQUEROR
CONAN THE AVENGER
CONAN OF AQUILONIA
CONAN OF THE ISLES
CONAN THE SWORDSMAN
CONAN THE LIBERATOR

Illustrated CONAN novels:

CONAN AND THE SORCERER
CONAN: THE FLAME KNIFE
CONAN THE MERCENARY
THE TREASURE OF TRANICOS

Other CONAN novels:

THE BLADE OF CONAN
THE SPELL OF CONAN

CONAN
THE
LIBERATOR

*L. Sprague de Camp
and Lin Carter*

14

ACE BOOKS, NEW YORK

CONAN THE LIBERATOR

An Ace Fantasy Book / published by arrangement with
Conan Properties, Inc.

PRINTING HISTORY
Sphere edition published 1980
Previously published by Bantam Books
Ace Fantasy edition / July 1987

ISBN: 0-441-11617-5

Ace Fantasy Books are published by The Berkley Publishing Group,
200 Madison Avenue, New York, New York 10016.
PRINTED IN THE UNITED STATES OF AMERICA

Contents

Introduction

Conan the Cimmerian, hero of heroes, was first conceived by Robert Ervin Howard (1906–36) of Cross Plains, Texas. Howard was an active pulp writer, and his career coincided with the greatest expansion of the pulp-magazine field. There were scores of such periodicals, all in the same format (about 6·5 × 10 inches) and printed on greyish uncoated paper. Now these magazines have disappeared, save for a few that still carry the old titles under a different format.

During the brief decade of his writing career, Howard wrote fantasy, science fiction, Westerns, sport stories, detective stories, historical fiction, stories of Oriental adventure, and verse. But of all his heroes, the one with the widest appeal is Conan the Cimmerian. In the genre of fantasy, the Conan stories have made Howard's work second only to that of J. R. R. Tolkien in popularity.

Born in Peaster, Texas, Howard lived all his short life in that state except for brief visits to adjacent states and to Mexico. His father was a frontier physician from Arkansas; a man of brusque, domineering manner, he was well regarded as an able country doctor. Robert Howard's mother, born in Dallas, Texas, thought herself socially above her husband and, for that matter, above all the folk of Cross Plains, where the family settled in 1919.

Both parents, but more especially the mother, were extremely possessive towards their only child. When Robert was a boy, his mother kept a vigilant watch over him and decided what friendships to permit him. When he grew to manhood, she actively discouraged any interest on his part in girls, although he did manage to date one young woman, a teacher, frequently during his last two years. Robert grew up slavishly devoted to his intermittently sickly mother; when he bought an automobile, he took her with him on long trips around Texas.

Puny and bullied as a small boy, Robert matured into a large, powerful man. He weighed nearly two hundred pounds, most of it muscle. He kept himself in shape by bag punching and weight lifting. His favourite sport, both active and passive, was boxing; he also became a football fan. Despite his rugged exterior, Robert Howard was a voracious bookworm. A fast and omnivorous reader, he would race through an entire shelf in a public library in a few hours.

While still an adolescent, he determined to pursue a writing career. When in 1928 he finished one year of noncredit courses at Howard Payne Academy in Brownwood, Texas, his father agreed to let him try freelance writing for a year before putting pressure on him to get a more conventional job. At the end of that time his sales, while modest, had been encouraging enough for his family to let him follow his bent.

Robert also grew up extremely moody, alternating between moments of wit, charm and spellbinding garrulity and spells of black depression, despair and misanthropy. He was hardly out of adolescence when he became fascinated with suicide. This obsession grew and deepened all his life. By hints and casual remarks, he let his parents and several friends know that he did not intend to survive his mother; but nobody took these veiled threats seriously.

In 1936, Robert Howard was a leading pulp writer with the best earnings of any man in Cross Plains. He enjoyed good health and had a congenial occupation, an adequate income, a growing circle of friends and admirers, and a promising literary future. But his mother lay dying of tuberculosis. When he learned that she was in a terminal coma, he went out, got into his car, and shot himself through the head.

From 1926 to 1930, Robert Howard wrote a series of fantasies about a hero called Kull, a barbarian from lost Atlantis who becomes king of a mainland realm. Howard had only meagre success with these stories; of the nine Kull stories he completed, he sold only three. These appeared in *Weird Tales*, a magazine of fantasy and science fiction published from 1923 to 1954. Although its word rates were low and its payments often late, *Weird Tales* nevertheless proved Howard's most reliable market.

In 1932, after the unsold Kull stories had languished in the trunk that Howard used as a filing cabinet, he rewrote one of these stories, changing the protagonist to Conan and adding a supernatural element; 'The Phoenix on the Sword' was published in *Weird Tales* for December 1932. The story attained instant popularity, and for several years Conan stories occupied a large part of Howard's working time. Eighteen of these stories appeared during Howard's lifetime; others were either rejected or unfinished. In some late letters, Howard considered dropping Conan to devote all his time to Westerns.

Conan was both a development of King Kull and an idealization of Robert Howard himself – a picture of Howard as he would like to have been. Howard idealized barbarians and the barbarian life as did Rudyard Kipling, Jack London and Edgar Rice Burroughs, all of whom influenced Robert E. Howard. Conan is the rough, tough, rootless, violent, far-travelled, irresponsible adventurer, of gigantic strength and stature, that Howard – whose own life was quiet, reclusive, aloof and introverted – liked to imagine himself. Conan combines the qualities of the Texan frontier hero Bigfoot Wallace, Burroughs's Tarzan, and A. D. Howden Smith's Viking hero Swain, with a dash of Howard's own sombre moodiness.

Howard himself spoke, in a letter to H. P. Lovecraft, of Conan's having 'stalked full grown out of oblivion and set me to work recording the saga of his adventures . . . He is simply a combination of a number of men I have known . . . prize-fighters, gunmen, bootleggers, oil-field bullies, gamblers and honest workmen I have come in contact with, and combining them all, produced the amalgamation I call Conan the Cimmerian.'

After Howard's death, some of his stories were published posthumously in the pulp magazines. Then the paper shortage of the Second World War slaughtered the pulps, and the Conan stories were forgotten save by a small circle of enthusiasts. In the 1950s, a New York publisher issued the

Conan stories in small printings as a series of clothbound volumes.

The present writer became involved in this enterprise as a result of finding some unpublished Howard material in the hands of a New York literary agent and adapting it for publication as part of this series. A decade later I arranged for paperback publication of the whole series, including several new adventures of Conan written in collaboration with my colleagues Lin Carter and Björn Nyberg. For years we have toiled to accommodate our own styles to Howard's, with what success the reader must judge. The present novel, to which my wife Catherine Crook de Camp has contributed extensive editorial assistance, is the latest of these efforts.

Meanwhile Glenn Lord, literary agent for the Howard heirs, by clever and persistent detective work, tracked down the trunk containing Howard's papers, which had disappeared after his death. This cache included more Conan stories or fragments of stories. These were also incorporated in the series, the incomplete tales being finished by Carter or me. Lord also arranged publication of scores of Howard's non-Conan stories, some reprinted from the pulps and some previously unpublished. While Howard's posthumous success has been gratifying, those who have taken part in it cannot help a feeling of sadness that Howard himself did not live to enjoy it.

There are several explanations for the extraordinary surge in Robert Howard's posthumous popularity. Some attribute it to the *Zeitgeist*. Many readers have grown tired of the anti-heroes, the heavily subjective, psychological stories, and the focus on contemporary socioeconomic problems that coloured so much fiction in the 1950s and '60s. For a time it looked as if fantasy had become a casualty of the Machine Age; but the success of Tolkien's *The Lord of the Rings* three-decker showed that a revival of fantasy was due. The Conan stories were among the first in the genre to benefit from this revival, and since their publication they have begotten a host of imitations.

Equal credit for their success must go to Howard's own ability as a writer. He was a natural storyteller, and this is the *sine qua non* of fiction writing. With this talent, many of any writer's faults may be overlooked; without it, no other virtues make up the lack.

Although self-taught, Howard achieved a notable and distinctive style – taut, colourful, rhythmic and eloquent. While using adjectives but sparingly, he achieved effects of colour and movement by lavish use of active verbs and personification, as can be seen at the start of his one full-length Conan novel: 'Know, O Prince, that between the years when the oceans drank Atlantis and the gleaming cities . . . there was an Age undreamed of, when shining kingdoms lay spread across the world like blue mantles beneath the stars . . .' With Howard's perfervid imagination, ingenious plots, hypnotic style, headlong narrative drive, and the intensity with which he put himself into his characters, even his pulpiest tales – his boxing and Western stories – are fun to read.

The fifty-odd Conan stories so far published relate the life of Conan from adolescence to old age. As a stage for his hero to stride across, sword in hand, Howard invented a Hyborian Age, set twelve thousand years ago between the sinking of Atlantis and the rise of recorded history. He postulated that barbarian invasions and natural catastrophes destroyed all records of this era, save for fragments appearing in later ages as myths and legends. He assured his readers that this was a purely fictional construct, not to be taken as a serious theory of prehistory.

In the Hyborian Age, magic worked and supernatural beings stalked the earth. The western part of the main continent, whose outlines differed signally from those on the modern map, was divided among a number of kingdoms, modelled on various realms of real ancient and medieval history. Thus Aquilonia corresponds more or less to medieval France, with Poitain as its Provence; Zingara resembles Spain; Asgard and Vanaheim answer to Viking Scandinavia; Shem with its warring city-states echoes the ancient Near East; while Stygia is a fictional version of ancient Egypt.

Conan is a native of Cimmeria, a bleak, hilly, cloudy northern land whose people are proto-Celts. Conan (whose name is Celtic) arrives as a youth at the easterly kingdom of Zamora and for several years makes his living as a thief. Then he serves as a mercenary soldier, first in the Oriental realm of Turan and then in several Hyborian kingdoms. Forced to flee from Argos, he becomes a pirate along the coast of Kush, with a Shemitish she-pirate and a crew of black corsairs.

Later Conan serves as a mercenary in various lands. He adventures among the nomadic *kozaks* of the eastern steppes and the pirates of the Vilayet Sea, the larger predecessor of the Caspian. He becomes a chieftain among the hill tribes of the Himelian Mountains, co-ruler of a desert city south of Stygia, a pirate of the Barachan Isles, and captain of a ship of Zingaran buccaneers.

Eventually he resumes the trade of soldier in the service of Aquilonia, the mightiest Hyborian kingdom of them all. He defeats the savage Picts on the western frontier, rises to general, but is forced to flee the murderous intentions of the depraved and jealous King Numedides.

After further adventures, Conan (now about forty years old) is rescued from the coast of Pictland by a ship bearing the leaders of a revolt against the tyrannical and eccentric rule of Numedides. They have chosen Conan as commander-in-chief of the rebellion, and here the present story opens.

L. SPRAGUE DE CAMP

Villanova, Pennsylvania
July 1978

I

When Madness Wears the Crown

Night hovered on black and filmy wings above the spires of royal Tarantia. Along fog-silenced streets cressets burned with the feral eyes of beasts of prey in primal wilderness. Few there were who walked abroad on nights like this, although the veiled darkness was redolent with the scent of early spring. Those few whom dire necessity drove out of doors stole forth like thieves on furtive feet and tensed at every shadow.

On the acropolis, round which sprawled the Old City, the palace of many kings lifted its crenelated crest against the wan and pallid stars. This castled capitol crouched upon its hill like some fantastic monster out of ages past, glaring at the Outer City walls, whose great stones held it captive.

On glittering suite and marble hall within the sullen palace, silence lay as thick as dust in mouldering Stygian tombs. Servants and pages cowered behind locked doors, and none bestrode the long corridors and curving stairs except the royal guard. Even these scarred and battle-seasoned veterans were loath to stare too deeply into shadows and winced at every unexpected sound.

Two guards stood motionless before a portal draped in rich hangings of brocaded purple. They stiffened and blanched as an eerie, muffled cry escaped from the apartment. It sang a thin, pitiful song of agony, which pierced like an icy needle the stout hearts of the guardsmen.

'Mitra save us all!' whispered the guard on the left, through pinched lips pale with tension.

His comrade said naught, but his thudding heart echoed the fervent prayer and added: 'Mitra save us all, and the land as well . . .'

For they had a saying in Aquilonia, the proudest kingdom of the Hyborian world: 'The bravest cower when madness wears the crown.' And the king of Aquilonia was mad.

Numedides was his name, nephew and successor to Vilerus III and the scion of an ancient royal line. For six years the kingdom had groaned beneath his heavy hand. Superstitious, ignorant, self-indulgent and cruel was Numedides; but heretofore his sins were merely those of any royal voluptuary with a taste for soft flesh, the crack of the lash, and the cries of cringing supplicants. For some time Numedides had been content to let his ministers rule the people in his name while he wallowed in the sensual pleasures of his harem and his torture chamber.

All this had changed with the coming of Thulandra Thuu. Who he was, this lean, dark man of many mysteries, none could say. Neither knew they whence or why he had come into Aquilonia out of the shadowy East.

Some whispered that he was a Witchman from the mist-veiled land of Hyperboria; others, that he had crept from haunted shadows beneath the crumbling palaces of Stygia or Shem. A few even believed him a Vendhyan, as his name – if it truly were his name – suggested. Many were the theories; but no one knew the truth.

For more than a year, Thulandra Thuu had dwelt in the palace, living on the bounty of the king and enjoying the powers and perquisites of a royal favourite. Some said he was a philosopher, an alchemist seeking to transmute iron into gold or to concoct a universal panacea. Others called him a sorcerer, steeped in the black arts of goëtia. A few of the more progressive nobles thought him naught but a clever charlatan, avid for power.

None, though, denied that he had cast a spell over King Numedides. Whether his vaunted mastery of alchemical science with its lure of infinite wealth had aroused the king's cupidity, or whether he had in sooth enmeshed the monarch in a web of sorcerous spells, none could be sure. But all could see that Thulandra Thuu, not Numedides, ruled from the Ruby Throne. His slightest whim had now become the law. Even the king's chancellor, Vibius Latro, had been instructed to take orders from Thulandra as if they had issued from the king himself.

Meanwhile Numedides's conduct had grown increasing strange. He ordered the golden coinage in his treasury cast into statues of himself adorned with royal jewels, and oft held converse with the blossoming trees and nodding flowers that graced his garden walks. Woe unto any kingdom when the crown is worn by a madman – a madman who, moreover, is the puppet of a crafty and unscrupulous favourite, whether a genuine magician or clever mountebank!

Behind the brocaded hangings of the guarded portal lay a suite whose walls were hung with mystic purple. Here a bizarre tableau unfolded.

In a translucent sarcophagus of alabaster, the king lay as if in deepest slumber. His gross body was unclothed. Even in the slackness of repose, his form testified to a life besmirched with vicious self-indulgence. His skin was blotched; his moist lips sagged; and his eyes were deeply pouched. Above the edge of the coffin bulged his bloated paunch, obscene and toadlike.

Suspended by her ankles, a naked twelve-year-old girl hung head down above the open casket. Her tender flesh bore the marks of instruments of torture. These instruments now lay among the glowing embers in a copper brazier that stood before a thronelike chair of sable iron, inlaid with cryptic sigils wrought in softly glowing silver.

The girl's throat had been neatly cut, and now bright blood ran down her inverted face and bedrabbed her ash-blonde hair. The casket beneath the corpse was awash with steaming blood, and in this scarlet bath the corpulent body of King Numedides lay partially immersed.

Set in a precise ellipse around the sarcophagus, to illuminate its contents, stood nineteen massive candles, each as tall as a half-grown boy. These candles had been fashioned, so rumour ran among the palace servants, of tallow stripped from human cadavers. But none knew whence they came.

Upon the black iron throne brooded Thulandra Thuu, a slender man of ascetic build and, seemingly, of middle years. His hair, bound by a fillet of ruddy gold, wrought in the likeness of a wreath of intertwining serpents, was silver grey; and serpentine were his cold, thick-lidded eyes. His mien declared him a philosopher, but his unwinking stare bespoke the zealot.

The bones of his narrow face seemed moulded by a sculptor. His skin was dark as teakwood; and from time to time he moistened his thin lips with a darting, pointed tongue. His spare torso was confined by an ample length of mulberry brocade, wrapped round and round and draped across one shoulder, leaving the other bare and exposing to view both of his scrawny arms.

At intervals he raised his eyes from the ancient, python-bound tome that lay upon his lap to stare thoughtfully into the alabaster casket, wherein the bloated body of King Nume-dides rested in its bath of virgin's blood. Then, frowning, he would again return to the pages of his book. The parchment of this monstrous volume was inscribed in a spidery hand in a language unknown to scholars of the West. Row upon row of hooked and cursive characters marched down the page in columns. And many of the glyphs were writ in inks of emerald, amethyst and vermillion, unfaded by the passage of the years.

A water clock of gold and crystal, set on a nearby taboret, chimed with a silvery tinkle. Thulandra Thuu once more looked deep into the casket. The tight-lipped expression on his dark visage bore wordless testimony to the failure of his undertaking. The rich red bath of blood was darkening; the surface became dull with scum as vitality faded from the cooling fluid.

Abruptly the sorcerer rose and, with an angry gesture of frustration, hurled the book aside. It struck the hangings on the wall and fell open, face down upon the marble floor. Had anyone been present to study the inscription on the spine and understand its cryptic signary, he would have discovered that this arcane volume was entitled: *The Secrets of Immortality, According to Guchupta of Shamballah.*

Awakened from his hypnotic trance, King Numedides clambered out of the sarcophagus and stepped into a tub of flower-scented water. He wiped his coarse features with a thirsty towel while Thulandra Thuu sponged the blood from his heavy body. The sorcerer would allow no one, not even the king's tiring men, into his oratory during his magical operations; therefore he must himself attend to the cleansing and tiring of the monarch. The king stared into the brooding, hooded eyes of the magician.

'Well?' demanded Numedides hoarsely. 'What were the results? Did the *signum vitalis* enter my body when drained from that little brat?'

'Some, great king,' replied Thulandra Thuu in a toneless, staccato voice. 'Some – but not enough.'

Numedides grunted, scratching a hairy paunch with an unpared fingernail. The thick, curly hair of his belly, like that of his short beard, was rusty red, fading into grey. 'Well, shall we continue, then? Aquilonia has many girls whose kin would never dare report their loss, and my agents are adept.'

'Allow me to consider, O King. I must consult the scroll of Amendarath to make certain that my partial failure lies not in an adverse conjunction or opposition of the planets. And I fain would cast your horoscope again. The stars foretoken ominous times.'

The king, who had struggled into a scarlet robe, picked up a beaker of empurpled wine, upon which floated the crimson buds of poppies, and downed the exotic drink.

'I know, I know,' he growled. 'Troubles flaring at the border, plots afoot in half the noble houses . . . But fear not, my trepidatious thaumaturge! This royal house has lasted long and will survive long after you are dust.'

The king's eyes glazed and a small smile played at the corner of his mouth as he muttered: 'Dust – dust – all is dust.

All save Numedides.' Then seeming to recover himself, he demanded irritably: 'Can you not give answer to my question? Would you have another girl-child for your experiments?'

'Aye, O King,' replied Thulandra Thuu after a moment of reflection. 'I have bethought me of a refinement in the procedure that, I am convinced, will bring us to our goal.'

The king grinned broadly and thumped a hairy hand against the sorcerer's lean back. The unexpected blow staggered the slender mage. A flicker of anger danced across the alchemist's dark features and was instantly extinguished, as by an unseen hand.

'Good, sir magician!' roared Numedides. 'Make me immortal to rule forever this fair land, and I will give you a treasury of gold. Already I feel the stirrings of divinity – albeit I will not yet proclaim my theophany to my steadfast and devoted subjects.'

'But Majesty!' said the startled sorcerer, recovering his composure. 'The country's plight is of more moment than you appear to know. The people grow restless. There are signs of insurrection from the south and from the sea. I understand not –'

The king waved him aside. 'I've put down treasonous rascals oft ere this, and I shall counter them again.'

What the king dismissed as trifling inconveniences were, in truth, matters worthy of a monarch's grave concern. More than one revolt simmered along the western borders of Aquilonia, where the land was rent asunder by wars and rivalries among the petty barons. The populace groaned beneath their ruler's obduracy and cried out for relief from oppressive taxation and monstrous maltreatment by agents of the king. But the worries of the common folk concerned their monarch little; he turned a deaf ear to their cries.

Yet Numedides was not so wedded to his peculiar pleasures that he failed to mark the findings of his spies, collected for him by his able minister, Vibius Latro. The chancellor reported rumours of no less a leader of the commons than the rich and powerful Count Trocero of Poitain. Trocero was no man idly to be dismissed – not with his peerless force of armoured cavalry and a warlike, fiercely loyal people ready to rise at his beckoning.

'Trocero,' mused the king, 'must be destroyed, it's true; but he's too strong for open confrontation. We must needs seek out a skilful poisoner . . . Meanwhile, my faithful, hard-fisted Amulius Procas is stationed in the southern border region. He has crushed more than one arrogant landowner who dared turn revolutionary.'

Inscrutable were the cold black eyes of Thulandra Thuu. 'Omens of danger overwhelming to your general I read upon the face of heaven. We must concern ourselves – '

Numedides ceased to listen. His trancelike slumber, together with the stimulus of the poppied wine, had flogged his sensual appetite. His harem newly housed a delectable, full-breasted Kushite girl, and a torture – yet unnamed – was forming in his twisted brain.

'I'm off,' he said abruptly. 'Detain me not, lest I blast you with my shafts of lightning.'

The king pointed a taut forefinger at Thulandra Thuu and made a guttural sound. Then, roaring with boorish mirth, he pushed aside a panel behind the purple arras and slipped through. Thence a secret passage led to that part of the harem whispered of, with loathing, as the House of Pain and Pleasure. The sorcerer watched him go with the shadow of a smile and thoughtfully snuffed out the nineteen massive candles.

'O King of Toads,' he muttered in his unknown tongue. 'You speak the very truth, save that you have the characters reversed. Numedides shall crumble into dust, and Thulandra Thuu shall rule the West from an eternal throne, when Father Set and Mother Kali teach their loving son to wrest from the dark pages of the vast Unknown the secret of eternal life . . .'

The thin voice pulsed through the darkened chamber like the dry rustle of a serpent's scales, slithering over the pallid bones of murdered men.

II

The Lions Gather

Far south of Aquilonia, a slender war galley cleft the stormy waters of the Western Ocean. The ship, of Argossean lines, was headed shoreward, where the lights of Messantia glimmered through the twilight. A band of luminescent green along the western horizon marked the passing of the day; and overhead, the first stars of evening bejewelled the sapphire sky, then paled before the rising of the moon.

On the forecastle, leaning upon the rail above the bow, stood seven persons cloaked against chill bursts of spray that fountained as the bronzen ram rose and dipped, cleaving the waves asunder. One of the seven was Dexitheus, a calm-eyed, grave-faced man of mature years, dressed in the flowing robes of a priest of Mitra.

Beside him stood a broad-shouldered, slim-hipped nobleman with dark hair tinged with grey, who wore a silvered cuirass, on the breast of which the three leopards of Poitain were curiously worked in gold. This was Trocero, Count of Poitain, and his motif of three crimson leopards was repeated on the banner that fluttered from the foremast high above his head.

At Count Trocero's elbow, a younger man of aristocratic bearing, elegantly clad in velvet beneath a silvered shirt of mail, fingered his small beard. He moved quickly, and his ready smile masked with gaiety the metal of a seasoned and skilful soldier. This was Prospero, a former general of the Aquilonian army. A stout and balding man, wearing neither sword nor armour and unmindful of the failing light, worked sums with a stylus on a set of waxed tablets, braced against the rail. Publius had been the royal treasurer of Aquilonia before his resignation in despairing protest against his monarch's policies of unlimited taxation and unrestrained expenditure.

Nearby, two girls clutched the inconstant rail. One was Belesa of Korzetta, a noblewoman of Zingara, slender and exquisite and but recently come to womanhood. Her long black hair streamed in the sea-wind like a silken banner. Nestled against her in the curve of one arm, a pale, flaxen-haired child stared wide-eyed at the lights that rimmed the waterfront. An Ophirean slave, Tina had been rescued from a brutal master by the Lady Belesa, niece of the late Count Valenso. Mistress and slave, inseparable, had shared the moody count's self-exile in the Pictish wilderness.

Above them towered a grim-faced man of gigantic stature. His smouldering eyes of volcanic blue and the black mane of coarse, straight hair that brushed his massive shoulders suggested the controlled ferocity of a lion in repose. He was a Cimmerian, and Conan was his name.

Conan's sea boots, tight breeches and torn silken shirt disclosed his magnificent physique. These garments he had looted from the chests of the dead pirate admiral, Bloody Tranicos, where in a cave on a hill in Pictland, the corpses of Tranicos and his captains still sat around a table heaped with the treasure of a Stygian prince. The clothes, small for so large a man, were faded, ripped, and stained with dirt and blood; but no one looking at the towering Cimmerian and the heavy broadsword at his side would mistake him for a beggar.

'If we offer the treasure of Tranicos in the open market-place,' mused Count Trocero, 'King Milo may regard us with disfavour. Hitherto he has entreated us fairly; but when rumours of our hoard of rubies, emeralds, amethysts and such-like trinkets set in gold do buzz about his ears, he may decree that the treasure shall escheat to the crown of Argos.'

Prospero nodded. 'Aye, Milo of Argos loves a well-filled treasury as well as any monarch. And if we approach the goldsmiths and moneylenders of Messantia, the secret will be shouted about the town within an hour's time.'

'To whom, then, shall we sell the jewels?' asked Trocero.

'Ask our commander-in-chief,' Prospero laughed slyly. 'Correct me if I'm wrong, General Conan, but did you not once have acquaintance with – ah – '

Conan shrugged. 'You mean, was I not once a bloody pirate with a fence in every port? Aye, so I was; and that I might have once again become, had you not arrived in time to plant my feet on the road to respectability.' He spoke Aquilonian fluently but with a barbarous accent.

After a moment's pause, Conan continued: 'My plan is this. Publius shall go to the treasurer of Argos and recover the deposit advanced upon the usage of this galley, minus the proper fee. Meanwhile, I'll take our treasure to a discreet dealer whom I knew in former days. Old Varro always gave me a fair price for plunder.'

'Men say,' quoth Prospero, 'that the gems of Tranicos have greater worth than all the other jewels in all the world. Men such as he of whom you speak would give us but a fraction of their value.'

'Prepare for disappointment,' said Publius. 'The value of such baubles ever gains in the telling but shrinks in the selling.'

Conan grinned wolfishly. 'I'll get what I can, fear not. Remember I have often dealt beneath the counter. Besides, even a fraction of the treasure is enough to set swinging all the swords in Aquilonia.' Conan looked back at the quarter-deck, where stood the captain and the steersman.

'Ho there,' Captain Zeno!' he roared in Argossean. 'Tell your rowers that if they put us ashore ere the taverns shutter for the night, it's a silver penny apiece for them, above their promised wage! I see the lights of the pilot boat ahead.'

Conan turned back to his companions and lowered his voice. 'Now, friends, we must guard our tongues as concerns our riches. A stray word, overheard, might cost us the where-withal to buy the men we need. Forget it not!'

The harbour boat, a gig rowed by six burly Argosseans, approached the galley. In the bow a cloak-wrapped figure wagged a lantern to and fro, and the captain waved an answer to the signal. As Conan moved to go below and gather his possessions, Belesa laid a slender hand upon his arm. Her gentle eyes sought his face, and there was anguish in her voice.

'Do you still intend to send us to Zingara?' she asked.

'It is best to part thus, Lady. Wars and rebellions are no places for gentlewomen. From the gems I gave you, you should realize enough to live on, with enough to spare for your dowry. If you wish, I'll see to converting them to coin. Now I have matters to attend to in my cabin.'

Wordlessly, Belesa handed Conan a small bag of soft leather, containing the rubies that Conan had taken from a chest in the cave of Tranicos. As he strode aft along the catwalk to his cabin in the poop, Belesa watched him go. All that was woman within her responded to the virility that emanated from him, like heat from a roaring blaze. Could she have had her unspoken wish, there would have been no need for a dowry. But, ever since Conan had rescued her and the girl Tina from the Picts, he had been to them no more than a friend and protector.

Conan, she realized with a twinge of regret, was wiser than she in such matters. He knew that a delicate, high-born lady, imbued with Zingaran ideals of womanly modesty and purity, could never adapt herself to the wild, rough life of an adventurer. Moreover, if he were slain or if he tired of her, she would become an outcast, for the princely houses of Zingara would never admit a barbarian mercenary's drab into their marble halls.

With a small sigh, she touched the girl who nestled beside her. 'Time to go below, Tina, and gather our belongings.'

Amid shouts and hails, the slender galley inched up to the quay. Publius paid the harbour tax and rewarded the pilot. He settled his debt to Captain Zeno and his crew and, reminding him of the secrecy of the mission, bade the Argossean skipper a ceremonious farewell.

As the captain barked his orders, the sail was lowered to the deck and stowed beneath the catwalk; the oars were shipped amid oaths and clatter and placed under the benches. The crew – officers, sailors and rowers – streamed merrily ashore, where bright lights blazed in inns and taverns; and painted slatterns, beckoning from second-storey windows, exchanged raillery and cheerful obscenities with the expectant mariners.

Men loitered about the waterfront street. Some lurched drunkenly along the roadway, while others snored in doorways or relieved themselves in the dark mouths of alleys.

One among the loiterers was neither so drunk nor so bleary-eyed as he appeared. A lean, hatchet-faced Zingaran he was, who called himself Quesado. Limp blue-black ringlets framed his narrow face, and his heavy-lidded eyes gave him a deceptive look of sleepy indolence. In shabby garments of sober black, he lounged in a doorway as if time itself stood still; and when accosted by a pair of drunken mariners, he retorted with a well-worn jest that sent them chuckling on their way.

Quesado closely observed the galley as it tied up to the quay. He noted that, after the crew had roistered off, a small group of armed men accompanied by two women disembarked and paused as they reached the pier, until several loungers hurried up to proffer their services. Soon the curious party disappeared, followed by a line of porters with chests and sea bags slung across their shoulders or balanced on their heads.

When darkness had swallowed up the final porter, Quesado sauntered over to a wineshop, where several crewmen from the ship had gathered. He found a cosy place beside the fire, ordered wine, and eyed the seamen. Eventually he chose a muscular, sunburned Argossean rower, already in his cups, and struck up a conversation. He bought the youth a jack of ale and told a bawdy jest.

The rower laughed uproariously, and when he had ceased chuckling, the Zingaran said indifferently: 'Aren't you from that big galley moored at the third pier?'

The Argossean nodded, gulping down his ale.

'Merchant galley, isn't she?'

26

The rower jerked back his tousled head and stared contemptuously. 'Trust a damned foreigner not to know one ship from another!' he snorted. 'She's a ship-o'-war, you spindle-shanked fool! That's the *Arianus*, pride of King Milo's navy.'

Quesado clapped a hand to his forehead. 'Oh, gods, how stupid of me! She's been abroad so long I scarce recognized her. But when she put in, was she not flying some device with lions on it?'

'Those be the crimson leopards of Poitain, my friend,' the oarsman said importantly. 'And the Count of Poitain, no less, hired the ship and himself commanded her.'

'I can scarcely credit it!' exclaimed Quesado, acting much amazed. 'Some weighty diplomatic mission, that I'll warrant . . .'

The drunken rower, puffed by the wind of his hearer's rapt attention, rushed on: 'We've been on the damndest voyage – a thousand leagues or more – and it's a wonder we didn't get our throats cut by the savage Picts –'

He broke off as a hard-faced officer from the *Arianus* clapped a heavy hand upon his shoulder.

'Hold your tongue, you babbling idiot!' snapped the mate, glancing suspiciously at the Zingaran. 'The captain warned us to keep close-mouthed, especially with strangers. Now shut your gob!'

'Aye, aye,' mumbled the rower. Avoiding Quesado's eye, he buried his face in his jack of ale.

'It's naught to me, mates,' yawned Quesado with a careless shrug. 'Little has happened in Messantia of late, so I but thought to nibble on some gossip.' He rose lazily to his feet, paid up, and sauntered out the door.

Outside, Quesado lost his air of sleepy idleness. He strode briskly along the pierside street until he reached a seedy roominghouse wherein he rented a chamber that overlooked the harbour. Moving like a thief in the night, he climbed the narrow stairs to his second-storey room.

Swiftly he bolted the door behind him, drew tattered curtains across the dormer windows, and lit a candle stub from the glowing coals in a small iron brazier. Then he hunched over a rickety table, forming tiny letters with a fine-pointed quill on a slender strip of papyrus.

His message written, the Zingaran rolled up the bit of flattened reed and cleverly inserted it into a brazen cylinder no larger than a fingernail. Then he scrambled to his feet, thrust open a cage that leaned against the seaward wall, and brought out a fat, sleepy pigeon. To one of its feet he secured the tiny cylinder; and gliding to the window, he drew aside the drape, opened the pane, and tossed the bird out into the night. As it circled the harbour and vanished, Quesado smiled, knowing that his carrier pigeon would find a safe roost and set out on its long journey northward with the coming of the dawn.

In Tarantia, nine days later, Vibius Latro, chancellor to King Numedides and chief of his intelligence service, received the brass tube from the royal pigeon-keeper. He unrolled the fragile papyrus with careful fingers and held it in the narrow band of sunlight that slanted through his office window. He read:

The Count of Poitain, with a small entourage, has arrived from a distant port on a secret mission. Q.

There is a destiny that hovers over kings, and signs and omens presage the fall of ancient dynasties and the doom of mighty realms. It did not require the sorceries of such as Thulandra Thuu to sense that the house of Numedides stood in grave peril. The signs of its impending fall were everywhere.

Messages came out of Messantia, travelling northward by dusty roads and by the unseen pathways of the air. To Poitain and the other feudal demesnes along the troubled and strife-torn borders of Aquilonia, these missives found their way; some even penetrated the palisaded camps and fortresses of the loyal Aquilonian army. For stationed there were swordsmen and pikemen, horsemen and archers who had served with Conan when he was an officer of King Numedides – men who had fought at Conan's side in the great battle of Velitrium, and even before that, at Massacre Meadow, when Conan first broke the hosts of savage Picts – men of his old regiment, the Lions, who well remembered him. And like the beasts whose name they bore, they remained loyal to the leader of the pride. Others who harkened to the call were wearied of service to a royal maniac who shrugged aside the business of his kingdom to indulge his unnatural lusts and to pursue mad dreams of eternal life.

In the months after Conan's arrival in Messantia, many Aquilonian veterans of the Pictish wars resigned or deserted from their units and drifted south to Argos. With them down the long and lonesome roads tramped Poitanians and Bossonians, Gundermen from the North, yeomen of the Tauran, petty nobles from Tarantia, impoverished knights from distant provinces, and many a penniless adventurer.

'Whence come they all?' marvelled Publius as he stood with Conan near the large tent of the commander-in-chief, watching a band of ragtail knights ride into the rebel camp. Their horses were lean, their trappings ragged, their armour rusty, and they were caked with dust and dried mud. Some bore bandaged wounds.

'Your mad king has made many enemies,' grumbled Conan. 'I get reports of knights whose lands he has seized, nobles whose wives or daughters he has outraged, sons of merchants whom he has stripped of their pelf – even common workmen and peasants, stout-hearted enough to take up arms against the royal madman. Those knights yonder are outlaws driven into exile for speaking out against the tyrant.'

'Tyranny oft breeds its own downfall,' said Publius. 'How many have we now?'

'Over ten thousand, by yesterday's reckoning.'

Publius whistled. 'So many? We had better limit our recruits ere they devour all the coin in our treasury. Vast as is the sum that you obtained for the jewels of Tranicos, 'twill melt like snow in the springtime if we enlist more men than we can afford to pay.'

Conan clapped the stout civilian on the back. 'It's your task as treasurer, good Publius, to make our purse outlast this feast of vultures. Only today I importuned King Milo for more camp space. Instead, he drenched me with a cataract of complaints. Our men crowd Messantia; they overtax the facilities of the city; they drive up prices; some commit crimes against the citizens. He wants us hence, either to a new camp or on our way to Aquilonia.'

Publius frowned. 'Whilst our troops train, we must remain close to the city and the sea, for access to supplies. Ten thousand men grow exceeding hungry when drilled as you drill them. And ten thousand bellies require much food, or their owners grow surly and desert.'

Conan shrugged. 'No help for it. Trocero and I ride forth on the morrow to scout for a new site. The next full moon should see us on the road to Aquilonia.'

'Who is that?' murmured Publius, indicating a soldier who, released from the morning's drill, was sauntering by, close to the general's tent. The man, clad in shabby black, had swilled a tankardful that afternoon; for his lean legs wobbled beneath him, and once he tripped over a stone that lay athwart his path. Sighting Conan and Publius, he swept off his battered cap, bowed so low that he quite unbalanced himself, recovered, and proceeded on his way.

Conan said: 'A Zingaran who turned up at the recruiting tent a few days past. He seemed a mousey little fellow – no warrior – but he has proved a fair swordsman, an excellent horseman, and an artist with a throwing knife; so Prospero signed him on with all the rest. He called himself – I think it was Quesado.'

'Your reputation, like a lodestone, draws men from near and far,' said Publius.

'So I had better win this war,' replied Conan. 'In the old days, if I lost a battle, I could slip away to lands that knew me not and start over again with nobody the wiser. That were not so easy now; too many men have heard of me.'

''Tis good news for the rest of us,' grinned Publius, 'that fame robs leaders of the chance to flee.'

Conan said nothing. Parading through his memory marched the arduous years since he had plunged out of the wintry

North, a ragged, starveling youth. He had warred and wandered the length and breadth of the Thurian continent. Thief, pirate, bandit, primitive chieftain – all these he had been; and common soldier, too, rising to general and falling again with the ebb of Fortune. From the savage wilderness of Pictland to the steppes of Hyrkania, from the snows of Nordheim to the steaming jungles of Kush, his name and fame were legend. Hence warriors flocked from distant lands to serve beneath his banner.

Conan's banner now proudly rode the breeze atop the central pole of the general's tent. Its device, a golden lion rampant on a field of sable silk, was Conan's own design. Son of a Cimmerian blacksmith, Conan was not at all of armigerous blood; but he had gained his greatest recognition as commander of the Lion Regiment in the battle at Velitrium. Its ensign he had adopted as his own, knowing that soldiers need a flag to fight for. It was following this victory that King Numedides, holding the Cimmerian's fame a threat to his own supremacy, had sought to trap and destroy his popular general, in whom he sensed a potential rival. Conan's growing reputation for invincibility he envied; his magnetic leadership he feared.

After eluding the snare Numedides had set for him, thus forfeiting his command, the Cimmerian looked back upon his days with the Lions with fond nostalgia. And now the banner under which he had won his mightiest victories flew above his head again, a symbol of his past glories and a rallying point for his cause.

He would need even mightier victories in the months ahead, and the golden lion on a field of black was to him an auspicious omen. For Conan was not without his superstitions. Although he had brawled and swaggered over half the earth, exploring distant lands and the exotic lore of foreign peoples, and had gained wisdom in the ways of kings and priests, wizards and warriors, magnates and beggars, the primitive beliefs of his Cimmerian heritage still smouldered in the depths of his soul.

Meanwhile, the spy Quesado, having passed beyond the purlieu of the commander's tent, miraculously regained his full sobriety. No longer staggering, he walked briskly along the rutted road towards the North Gate of Messantia.

The spy had prudently retained his waterfront room when he took up soldier's quarters in the tent city outside the walls. And in that room, pushed under the rough-hewn door, he found a letter. It was unsigned, but Quesado knew the hand of Vibius Latro.

Having fed his pigeons, Quesado sat down to decipher the simple code that masked the meaning of the message. It seemed a jumble of domestic trivia; but, by marking every fourth word, Quesado learned that his master had sent him an accomplice. She was, the letter said, a woman of seductive beauty.

Quesado allowed himself a thin, discreet smile. Then he penned his usual report on a slender strip of papyrus and sent it winging north to far Tarantia.

While the army drilled, sweated, and increased in size, Conan bade farewell to the Lady Belesa and her youthful protégée. He saw their carriage go rattling off along the coastal road to Zingara, with a squad of sturdy guards riding before and behind. Hidden in the baggage, an iron-bound box enclosed sufficient gold to keep Belesa and Tina in comfort for many years, and Conan hoped that he would see no more of them.

Although the burly Cimmerian was sensible of Belesa's charms, he intended at this point to become entangled with no woman, least of all with a delicate gentlewoman, for whom there was no place in the wardrooms of war. Later, should the rebellion triumph, he might require a royal marriage to secure his throne. For thrones, however high their cost in common blood, must ofttimes be defended by the mystic power engendered by the blood of kings.

Still, Conan felt the pangs of lust no less than any active, virile man. Long had he been without a woman, and he showed his deprivation by curt words, sullen moods and stormy explosions of temper. At last Prospero, divining the cause of these black moods, ventured to suggest that Conan might do well to set his eyes upon the tavern trulls of Messantia.

'With luck and discernment, General,' he said, 'you could find a bedmate to your fancy.'

Prospero was unaware that his words buzzed like horse-flies in the ears of a lank Zingaran mercenary, who huddled nearby with his back against a tent-stake, head bowed forward on his knees, apparently asleep.

Conan, equally unmindful, shrugged off his friend's suggestion. But as the days passed, desire battled with his self-control. And with every passing night, his need waxed more compelling.

Day by day, the army grew. Archers from the Bossonian Marches, pikemen from Gunderland, light horse from Poitain, and men of high and low degree from all of Aquilonia streamed in. The drill field resounded to the shouts of commands, the tramp of infantry, the thunder of cavalry, the snap of bowstrings and the whistle of arrows. Conan, Prospero and Trocero laboured ceaselessly to forge their raw recruits into a well-trained army. But whether this force, cobbled together from far-flung lands and never battle-tested, could withstand the crack troops of the hard-riding, hard-fighting and victorious Amulius Procas, no man knew.

Meanwhile, Publius organised a rebel spy service. His agents penetrated far into Aquilonia. Some merely sought for news. Some spread reports of the depravity of King Numedides – reports which the rumourmongers found needed no exaggeration. Some begged for monetary aid from nobles who, while sympathetic to the rebel cause, had not yet dared declare themselves in favour of rebellion.

Each day, at noon, Conan reviewed his troops. Then, in rotation, he took his midday meal in the mess tent of each company; for a good leader knows many of his men by name and strengthens their loyalty by personal contact. A few days after Prospero's talk about the public women of Messantia, Conan dined with a company of light cavalry. He sat among the common soldiers and traded bawdy jests as he shared their meat, bread and bitter ale.

At the sound of a sibilant voice, suddenly upraised, Conan turned his head. Nearby, a narrow-faced Zingaran, whom Conan remembered having seen before, was orating with grandiloquent gestures. Conan left a joke caught in an endless pause and listened closely; for the fellow was talking about women, and Conan felt a stirring in his blood.

'There's a certain dancing girl,' cried the Zingaran, 'with hair as black as a raven's wing and eyes of emerald green. And there is a witchery in her soft red lips and in her limber body, and her breasts are like ripe pomegranates!' Here he cupped the ambient air with mobile hands.

'Every night she dances for thrown coppers at the Inn of the Nine Swords and bares her swaying body to the eyes of men. But she is a rare one, this Alcina – a haughty, fastidious minx who denies to all men her embrace. She has not met the man who could arouse her passion – or so she claims.

'Of course,' added Quesado, winking lewdly, 'there are doubtless lusty warriors in this very tent who could woo and win that haughty lass. Why, our gallant general himself –'

At that instant Quesado caught Conan's eye upon him. He broke off, bent his head, and said: 'A thousand pardons, noble general! Your excellent beer so loosened my poor tongue that I forgot myself. Pray, ignore my indiscretion, I beg you, my good lord –'

'I'll forget it,' growled Conan and turned back frowning to his food.

But that very evening, he asked his servants for the way to an inn called the Nine Swords. As he swung into the saddle and, with a single mounted groom for escort, pounded off towards the North Gate, Quesado, skulking in the shadows, smiled a small, complacent smile.

III

Emerald Eyes

When dawn came laughing to the azure sky, a silver-throated trumpet heralded the arrival of an envoy from King Milo. Brave in embroidered tabard, the herald trotted into the rebel camp on a bay mare, brandishing aloft a sealed and beribboned scroll. The messenger sniffed disdainfully at the bustling drill ground, where a motley host was lining up for roll call. When he thundered his demand for escort to General Conan's tent, one of Trocero's men led the beast towards the centre of the camp.

'This means trouble,' murmured Trocero to the priest Dexitheus as they gazed after the Argossean herald.

The lean, bald Mitran priest fingered his beads. 'We should be used to trouble by now, my lord Count,' he replied. 'And much more trouble lies ahead, as well you know.'

'You mean Numedides?' asked the count with a wry smile. 'My good friend, for that kind of trouble we are ready. I speak of difficulties with the King of Argos. For all that he gave me leave to muster here, I feel that Milo grows uneasy with so many men, pledged to a foreign cause, encamped outside his capital. Meseems His Majesty begins to repent him of his offer of a comfortable venue for our camp.'

'Aye,' added Publius, as the stout paymaster strolled up to join the other two. 'I doubt not that the stews and alleys of Messantia already crawl with spies from Tarantia. Numedides will put a subtle pressure on the King of Argos to persuade him to turn against us now.'

'The king were a fool to do so,' mused Trocero, 'with our army close by and lusting for a fight.'

Publius shrugged. 'The monarch of Messantia has hitherto been our friend,' he said. 'But kings are given to perfidy, and expediency rules the hearts of even the noblest of them. We must needs wait and see . . . I wonder what ill news that haughty herald bore?'

Publius and Trocero strolled off to attend their duties, leaving Dexitheus absently fingering his prayer beads. When he had spoken of future troubles, he thought not only of the coming clash but also of another portent.

The night before, his slumbers had been roiled by a disturbing dream. Lord Mitra often granted his loyal suppliants foreknowledge of events through dreams, and Dexitheus wondered if his dream had been a prophecy.

In this dream, General Conan confronted the enemy on a battlefield, harking on his soldiers with brandished sword; but behind the giant Cimmerian lurked a shadowy form, slender and furtive. Naught could the sleeper discern of this stealthy presence save that in its hood-shadowed visage burned catlike eyes of emerald green, and that it ever stood at Conan's unprotected back.

Although the risen sun had warmed the mild spring morning, Dexitheus shivered. He did not like such dreams; they cast pebbles into the deep well of his serenity. Besides, no recruit in the rebel camp had eyes of such a brilliant green, or he would have noticed the oddity.

Along the dusty road back to Messantia cantered the herald, as messengers went forth to summon the leaders of the rebel host to council.

In his tent, the giant Cimmerian barely checked his anger as his squires strapped him into his harness for his morning exercise with arms. When Prospero, Trocero, Dexitheus, Publius and the others were assembled, he spoke sharply, biting off his words.

'Briefly, friends,' he rumbled, 'it is His Majesty's pleasure that we withdraw north to the grassy plains, at least nine leagues from Messantia. King Milo feels our nearness to his capital endangers both his city and our cause. Some of our troops, quoth he, have been enjoying themselves a bit too rowdily of late, shattering the king's peace and giving trouble to the civic guard'

'I feared as much,' sighed Dexitheus. 'Our warriors are much given to the pleasures of the goblet and the couch. Still and all, it asks too much of human nature to expect soldiers – especially a mixed crowd like ours – to behave with the meekness of hooded monks.'

'True,' said Trocero. 'And luckily we are not unprepared to go. When shall we move, General?'

Conan buckled his sword belt with a savage gesture. His blue eyes glared lionlike beneath his square-cut black mane.

'He gives us ten days to be gone,' he grunted, 'but I am fain to move at once. Messantia has too many eyes and ears to please me, and too many of our soldiery have limber tongues, which a stoup of wine sets wagging. I'll move, not nine leagues but ninety, from this nest of spies.

'So let's be off, my lords. Cancel all leaves and drag our men out of the wineshops, by force if need be. This night I shall proceed with a picked troop to study the route and choose a new campsite. Trocero, you shall command until I rejoin the army.'

They saluted and left. All the rest of that day, soldiers were rounded up, provisions readied, and gear piled into wagons. Before the next morning's sun had touched the gilded pinnacles of Messantia with its lances of light, tents were struck and companies formed for the line of march. While the ghosts of fog still floated on the lowlands, the army got under way – knight and yeoman, archer and pikeman, all well guarded by scouts and flankers before, behind, and on the sides.

Conan and his troop of Poitanian light horse had trotted off to northward, while darkness veiled the land. The barbarian general did not entirely trust King Milo's friendship. Many considerations mould the acts of kings; and Numedides's agents might have already persuaded the Argossean monarch to ally himself with the ruler of Aquilonia, rather than espouse the unpredictable fortunes of the rebels.

Surely Argos knew that, if the insurrection failed, Aquilonia's vengeance would be swift and devastating. And, if a king is bent upon destruction, an army is best attacked while on the march, with the men strung out and encumbered by their gear . . .

So the Lions moved north. Company by company, the unseasoned army tramped the dusty road, splashed across the fords of shallow rivers, and snaked through the low Didymian Hills. No one ambushed, attacked or harassed the marching men. Perhaps Conan's suspicions of King Milo were unjustified; perhaps the army was too strong for the Argosseans to try conclusions with them. Or perhaps the king awaited a more felicitous moment to hurl his strength against the rebels. Whether he were friend or secret foe, Conan rejoiced in his precautions.

When his forces had covered the first day's march without interference, Conan, cantering back from his chosen campsite, relaxed a little. They were now beyond the reach of the spies that infested the winding alleys of Messantia. His scouts and outriders travelled far and wide; if unfriendly eyes watched the army in the countryside, Conan looked to his scouts to sniff their owners out. None was discovered.

The giant Cimmerian trusted few men and those never lightly. His long years of war and outlawry had reinforced his feline wariness. Still, he knew these men who followed him, and his cause was theirs. Thus it never occurred to him that spies might be already in his camp and ill-wishers at his very back.

Two days later, the rebels forded the River Astar in Hypsonia and entered the Plain of Pallos. To the north loomed the Rabirian Mountains, a serrated line of purple peaks marching like giants into the sunset. The army made its camp at the edge of the plain, on a low, rounded hillock that would offer some protection when fortified around the top by ditch and palisade. Here, so long as supplies came regularly from

Messantia or from nearby farms, the warriors could perfect their skills before crossing the Alimane into Poitain, the southernmost province of Aquilonia.

During the long day after their arrival, the grumbling soldiers laboured with pick, shovel and mattock to surround the camp with a protective rampart. Meanwhile a troop of light horse cantered back along the road by which they had come, to escort the plodding supply wagons.

But during the second watch of that night, a slender figure glided from the darkness of Conan's tent into a pool of moonlight. It was robed and muffled in a long, full caftan of amber wool, which blended into the raw earth beneath its feet. This figure came upon another, shrouded in the shadow of a nearby tent.

The two exchanged a muttered word of recognition. Then slim, beringed fingers pressed a scrap of parchment into the other's labour-grimed hands.

'On this map I have marked the passes that the rebels will take into Aquilonia,' said the girl in the silken, sibilant whisper of a purring cat. 'Also the disposition of the regiments.'

'I'll send the word,' murmured the other. 'Our master will see that it gets to Procas. You have done well, Lady Alcina.'

'There is much more to do, Quesado,' said the girl. 'We must not be seen together.'

The Zingaran nodded and vanished into the darkest shadows. The dancer threw back her hood and looked up at the argent moon. Although she had just come from the lusty arms of Conan the Cimmerian, her moonlit features were icily unmoved. Like a mask carved from yellow ivory was that pallid oval face; and in the cool depths of her emerald eyes lurked traces of amusement, malice and disdain.

That night, as the rebel army slept upon the Plain of Pallos in the embrace of the Rabirian Mountains, one recruit deserted. His absence was not discovered until roll call the next morning; and when it was, Trocero deemed it a matter of small moment. The man, a Zingaran named Quesado, was reputedly a lazy malingerer whose loss would be of little consequence.

Despite his feckless manner, Quesado was in truth anything but lazy. The most diligent of spies, he masked with seeming indolence his busy watching, listening, and compiling of terse but accurate reports. And that night, while the encampment slumbered, he stole a horse from the paddock, eluded the sentinels, and galloped northward hour after weary hour.

Ten days later, splashed with mud, covered with dust, and staggering with exhaustion, Quesado reached the great gates of Tarantia. The sight of the sigil he wore above his heart gained him swift access to Vibius Latro, Numedides's chancellor.

The master of spies frowned over the map that Alcina had slipped into Quesado's hand and that the Zingaran now handed to him. Sternly he asked:

'Why did you bring it yourself? You know you are needed with the rebel army.'

The Zingaran shrugged. 'It was impossible to send it by carrier pigeon, my lord. When I joined that gaggle of rebels, I had to leave my birds in Messantia, under care of my replacement, Fadius the Kothian.'

Vibius Latro stared coldly. 'Then, why did you not take the map to Fadius, who could have flown it hither in the accustomed manner? You could have remained in that nest of traitors to follow the winds of change. I counted on your knife at Conan's back.'

Quesado gestured helplessly. 'When the lady Alcina obtained this copy of the map, Master, the army was already three days' ride beyond Messantia. I could scarce request a six-day leave to go thither and return without arousing suspicion, whilst to go as a deserter would have meant searches and questions by the Argosseans. Nor could I rejoin the army once I had departed without leave. And pigeons do betimes get lost, or are slain by falcons or wildcats or hunters. For a document of such moment, I deemed it better to carry it myself.'

The chancellor grunted, pursing his lips. 'Why, then, did you not bear it straightway to General Procas?'

Quesado was now perspiring freely. His sallow brow and bestubbled cheeks glistened with moisture. Vibius Latro was no man lightly to displease.

'General P-Procas knows me not.' The spy's voice grew querulous. 'My sigil would mean naught to him. Only you, my lord, command all channels for transmission of such intelligence to the military chiefs.'

A small, thin-lipped smile flickered across the other's enigmatic features. 'Quite so,' he said. 'You have done adequately. I should have liked it better had Alcina obtained the map ere the rebels marched north from Messantia.'

'Methinks the rebel leaders had not fully chosen their route before the night of my departure,' said Quesado. He did not know this for a fact, but it had a reasonable ring.

Vibius Latro dismissed the spy and summoned his secretary. Studying the map, he dictated a brief message to General Amulius Procas, with a copy for the king. While the secretary copied Alcina's crude sketch, Latro summoned a page and gave him both copies of each document.

'Take these to the king's secretary,' the chancellor said, 'and ask that His Majesty impress his seal upon one set. Then, if there be no objection, ride with that set to Amulius Procas in Poitain. Here is a pass to the royal stables. Choose the swiftest horse, and change mounts at each post inn.'

The message came not to the king's secretary. It was, instead, delivered into the thin, dark hands of Thulandra Thuu by his Khitan servant, Hsiao. As the king's sorcerer read the message and examined the map in the light of a corpse-fat candle, he smiled coldly, nodding approval to the Khitan.

'It fell out as you predicted, Master,' said Hsiao. 'I told the page that His Majesty and his scribe were closeted with you, so he handed the scrolls to me.'

'You have done well, good Hsiao,' said Thulandra Thuu.

41

'Fetch me the wax; I will seal the scrolls myself. There is no need to distract His Majesty from his pleasures for a trifle.'

From a locked coffer the sorcerer took a duplicate of the king's seal ring and, folding together one copy each of map and message, he lit a taper from one of the massive candles. Touching the sealing wax to the flame, he dripped the molten wax along the open edge of the packet. Thulandra then stamped the cooling wax with the duplicate seal ring and handed the package to the Khitan.

'Give this to Latro's courier,' he said, 'and tell him that His Majesty desires it to go post-haste to General Procas. Then draft me a letter to Count Ascalante of Thune, at present commanding the Fourth Tauranian Regiment at Palaea. I require his presence here.'

Hsiao hesitated. 'Dread lord!' he said.

Thulandra Thuu looked at his servant sharply. 'Well?'

'It is not unknown to this unworthy person that you and General Procas are not always in accord. Permit me to ask: Is it your wish that he shall triumph over the barbarian rebel?'

Thulandra Thuu smiled thinly. Hsiao knew that the wizard and the general were fierce rivals for the King's regard, and Hsiao was the only person in the world in whom the sorcerer was willing to confide. Thulandra murmured:

'For the time being. As long as Procas remains in the southern provinces, far from Tarantia, he cannot threaten my position here. And I must risk that he add another victory to his swollen list, since neither he nor I would welcome Conan at the gates of Tarantia.

'Procas stands betwixt the rebels and their march upon the capital. I intend that he shall crush the insurrection, aye; but in such wise that the credit shall fall to me. Then, perchance, an accident may take our heroic general from us in his moment of victory, ere he can return in triumph to Tarantia. Now be on your way.'

Hsiao bowed low and silently withdrew. Thulandra Thuu

unlocked a chest of ebony and placed therein his copies of
the documents.

Trocero stared in puzzlement at his commander, who paced
the tent like a caged tiger, angry impatience smouldering in
his fierce blue eyes.

'What ails you, General Conan?' he demanded. 'I thought
it was lack of a woman, but since you carried off the dancing
girl, that explanation is a punctured wineskin. What troubles
you?'

Conan ceased his restless pacing and came over to the
field table. Glowering, he poured himself a cup of wine.

'Naught that I can set a name to,' he growled. 'But of late
I grow fretful, starting at shadows.'

He broke off, eyes suddenly alert, as he stared into one
corner of the tent. Then he forced a gruff laugh and threw
himself back in his leather campaign chair.

'Crom, I'm as restless as a bitch in heat!' he said. 'For-
sooth, I know not what is gnawing at my vitals. Sometimes,
when we confer, I half believe that the very shadows listen
to our words.'

'Shadows do betimes have ears,' said Trocero. 'And eyes
as well.'

Conan shrugged. 'I know there be none here save you and
me, with the lass at rest, and my two squires burnishing my
armour, and the sentries tramping outside the tent,' he
muttered. 'Still and all, I sense a listening presence.'

Trocero did not scoff, and foreboding grew upon him.
He had learned to trust the Cimmerian's primitive instincts,
knowing them keener by far than those of civilized men like
himself.

But Trocero was not without instincts of his own; and
one of these bade him distrust the supple dancing girl whom
Conan had borne off as his willing mistress. Something about
her bothered Trocero, although he could not put his finger
on the reason. Certainly she was beautiful – if anything, too
beautiful to dance for thrown coppers in a Messantian pier-

side tavern. Also, she was too silent and secretive for his taste. Trocero could usually charm a woman into a babbling stream of confidences; but, when he had tried to draw Alcina out, he had no success at all. She answered his questions politely but concommittally, leaving him no wiser than before.

He shrugged, poured himself another cup, and consigned all such perturbations to the nine hells of Mitra. 'The inaction chafes you, Conan,' he said. 'Once we are on the march, with the Lion banner floating overhead, you'll feel yourself again. No more listening shadows then!'

'Aye,' grunted Conan.

What Trocero had said was true enough. Give Conan an enemy of flesh and blood, put cold steel in his hand, and he would dare the deadliest odds with a high heart. But, when he strove against impalpable foes and insubstantial shadows, the primitive superstitions of his tribal ancestors crowded into his mind.

In the rear of the tent, behind a curtain, Alcina smiled a slow, catlike smile, while her slim fingers played with a curious talisman, which hung by a delicate chain about her neck. There was only one match to it in all the world.

Far to the north, beyond the plains and the mountains and the River Alimane, Thulandra Thuu sat upon his wrought-iron throne. On his lap, partly unrolled, he held a scroll inscribed with astrological diagrams and symbols. Before him on a taboret stood an oval mirror of black volcanic glass. From one edge of this mystic mirror, a semicircular chip was missing, and it was this half-disc of obsidian, bound to the main glass by subtle linkages of psychic force, that hung between the rounded breasts of Alcina the dancing girl.

As the sorcerer studied the chart on his knee, he raised his head betimes to glance at the small water clock of gilt and crystal, which stood beside the mirror. From this rare instrument came a steady drip, drip, inaudible to all but the keenest ears.

When the silver bell within the clock chimed the hour, Thulandra Thuu released the scroll. He moved a clawlike

44

hand before the mirror, muttering an exotic charm in an unknown tongue. Gazing into the mirror's depths, he became one in mind and soul with his servant, the lady Alcina; for when a mystic trance linked the twain, at a moment determined by certain aspects of the heavenly bodies, the sights Alcina saw and the words she uttered were transmitted magically to the sorcerer in Tarantia.

Truly, the mage had little need of the men of Vibius Latro's corps of spies. And truly Conan's keen senses served him well: even the shadows in his tent had eyes and ears.

IV

The Bloody Arrow

Each dawn the brazen trumpets routed the men from slumber to drill for hours upon the Plain of Pallos and, with the setting sun, dismissed them to their night's repose; and still the army grew. And with the newcomers came news and gossip from Messantia. The moon had shrunk from a silver coin to a sickle of steel when the captains of the rebellion gathered in Conan's tent for supper. After washing down their coarse campaign fare with draughts of weak green beer, the leaders of the host consulted.

'Daily,' mused Trocero, 'it seems King Milo grows more restive.'

Publius nodded. 'Aye, it pleases him not to have within his borders so great an armed force, under another's leadership. Be like he fears that we shall turn upon him, as easier prey than the Aquilonian tyrant.'

Dexitheus, priest of Mitra, smiled. 'Kings are a suspicious lot at best, ever fearful for their crowns. King Milo is no different from the rest.'

'Think you he'll seek to attack us in the rear?' growled Conan.

The black-robed priest turned up a narrow hand. 'Who can say? Even I, trained by my holy office to read the hearts of men, dare hazard no guess as to the shrouded thoughts that lurk in King Milo's mind. But I advise that we cross the Alimane, and soon.'

'The army is prepared,' said Prospero. 'The men are trained and as ready to fight as ever they will be. It were well they were blooded soon, ere inaction dulls the edge of their fighting spirit.'

Conan nodded sombrely. Experience had taught him that

an army, over-trained and under-used, is often splintered into quarrelling factions by those same forces of pride and militancy that its trainers have so painstakingly instilled. Or it rots, like overripe fruit.

'I agree, Prospero,' said the Cimmerian. 'But an equal peril lies in too early a move. Surely Procas in Aquilonia has spies to tell him that we lodge in the mountains of northern Argos. And a general less shrewd than he would guess that we mean to cross the Alimane into Poitain, the most disaffected of all the provinces of Aquilonia. He needs but to mount a heavy guard at every ford and keep his Border Legion mobile, ready to march to any threatened crossing.'

Trocero swept back his greying hair with confident fingers. 'All Poitain will rise to march with us; but my partisans keep silent, lest word reach the vigilant Procas in time to act.'

The others exchanged significant glances, wherein hope and scepticism mingled. Days before, messengers had left the rebel camp to enter Poitain in the guise of merchants, tinkers and pedlars. Their mission was to urge Count Trocero's liege-men and supporters to prepare for forays and diversions, to confuse the royalists or to draw them off in futile pursuit of raiding bands. Once these agents had carried out their mission, a signal to move would reach the rebel army – a Poitanian arrow dipped in blood. Meanwhile, waiting for the message stretched nerves taut.

Prospero said: 'I am less concerned about the rising of Poitain, which is as certain as aught can be in this chancy world, than I am about the promised deputation from the northern barons. If we be not at Culario by the ninth day of the vernal month, they may withdraw, since planting time will be upon them.'

Conan grunted and drained his goblet. The northern lord-lings, in smouldering revolt against Numedides, had vowed to support the rebels but would not openly commit them-selves to a rebellion stigmatised by failure. If the Lion banner were broken at the Alimane, or if the Poitanian revolt failed to take fire, no bond would tie these self-serving nobles to the rebel cause.

The barons' caution was understandable; but uncertainty drove sharp spurs into the rebel leaders' souls. If they must linger on the Plain of Pallos until the Poitanians sent their secret signal, would there be time to reach Culario on the appointed day? Despite the headstrong urgings of his barbaric nature, Conan counselled patience until the Poitanian signal came. But his officers remained uncertain or offered divers plans.

So the rebel leaders argued far into the night. Prospero wished to split the army into three contingents and hurl them all at once upon the three best fords: those of Mevano, Nogara and Tunais.

Conan shook his head. 'Procas will expect just that,' he said.

'What, then?' Prospero frowned.

Conan spread the map and with a scarred forefinger pointed to the middle ford, Nogara. 'We'll feint here, with two or three companies only. You know tricks to convince the foe that our numbers are vaster than they truly are. We'll set up empty tents, light extra campfires, and parade companies within view of the foe and then swing them out of sight behind a copse and around the circuit again. We'll unlimber a couple of ballistas on the river bank to harass the crossing guards. Those screeching darts should entice Procas and his army thither in a hurry.

'You, Prospero, shall command the diversion,' Conan added. Learning that he would miss the main battle, the young commander began to object, but Conan silenced him: 'Trocero, you and I shall take the remaining troops, half to Mevano and the balance to Tunais, and force the two crossings. With luck, we may catch Procas in a nutcracker.'

'Perchance you're right,' murmured Trocero. 'With our Poitanians in revolt in Procas's rear . . .'

'May the gods smile upon your plan, General,' said Publius, mopping his brow. 'If not, all is lost!'

'Ah, gloomy one!' said Trocero. 'War is a chancy trade, and we have no less to lose than you. Win or lose, we all must stand together.'

'Aye, even at the foot of the gallows,' muttered Publius.

Behind the partition in Conan's tent, his mistress lay couched on a bed of furs, her slender body gleaming in the feeble light of a single candle, whose wavering flame reflected strangely in her emerald eyes and in the clouded depths of the small obsidian talisman that reposed in the scented valley of her breasts. She smiled a catlike smile.

Before dawn, Trocero was roused from his couch by the urgent hand of a sentry. The count yawned, stretched, blinked, and irritably struck the guard's hand aside.

'Enough!' he barked. 'I am awake, lout, though it scarcely seems light enough for roll call . . .'

His face went blank and his voice died as he saw what the guard held out to him. It was a Poitanian arrow, coated from barb to feathers with dried blood.

'How came this here?' he asked. 'And when?'

'A short time past, my lord Count, borne by a rider from the north,' replied the guard.

'So! Summon my squires! Sound the alarm and bear the arrow forthwith to General Conan!' cried Trocero, heaving himself to his feet.

The guard saluted and left. Soon two squires, knuckling sleep from their eyes, hastened in to attire the count and buckle on his armour.

'Action at last, by Mitra, Ishtar, and Crom of the Cimmerians!' cried Trocero. 'You there, Mnester! Summon my captains to council! And you, boy, has Black Lady been fed and watered? See to her saddling, and quickly. Draw the girth tight! I've no wish for a cold bath in the waters of the Alimane!'

Before a ruby sun inflamed the forested crests of the Rabirian Mountains, the tents were struck, the sentries recalled, and the wains laden. By the time bright day had chased away the laggard morning mists, the army was on the march in three long columns, heading for Saxula Pass through the mountains and beyond it for Aquilonia and war.

The land grew rugged and the road tortuous. On either side rose barren rondures toothed with stony outcrops. These were the foothills of the Rabirians, which scurried westward following the stately tread of the adjacent mountains.

Hour after hour, warriors and camp servants trudged up the long slopes and down the further sides. The hot sun beat upon them as they manhandled heavy vehicles over steep rises, clustering about the wains like bees around a hive to push, heave and pull. On the downward slopes, each teamster belayed one wheel with a length of chain, so that, unable to rotate, it served to brake the vehicle. Dust devils eddied skyward, besmudging the crystalline mountain air.

As they crested each rise, the main range receded miragelike before them. But, when the purple shadows of late afternoon fingered the eastern slope of every hill, the mountains opened out, like curtains drawn aside. They parted to disclose Saxula Pass, a deep cleft in the central ridge, as if made by a blow from an axe in the hand of an angry god.

As the army struggled upwards towards the pass, Conan commanded a contingent of his scouts to clamber up the steep sides of the opening to make sure no ambush awaited his coming. The scouts signalled that all was clear, and the army tramped on through. The footfalls of men, the rattle of equipment, the drum of hooves and the creak of axles reverberated from the rocky cliffs on either hand.

As the men emerged from the confines of the pass, the road wound downward, losing itself in the thick stands of cedar and pine that masked the northern slopes. In the distance, beyond the intermediate ranges, the men glimpsed the Alimane, coiling through the flatlands like a silvery serpent warmed by the last rays of the setting sun.

Down the winding slope they went, with wheels lashed to hold the wagons back. As the stars throbbed in the darkening sky, they reached a fork in the road beyond the pass. Here the army halted and set up camp. Conan flung his sentinels out wide, to guard against a night attack from the foe across the river. But nothing disturbed the weary troopers' rest except the snarl of a prowling leopard, which fled at a sentry's shout.

The following morning, Trocero and his contingent departed along the right branch of the fork, headed for the ford of Tunais. Conán and Prospero, with their forces, continued down the left branch until, shortly before noon, they reached another fork. Here Prospero with his small detachment bore to the right, for the central ford of Nogara. Conan, with the remaining horse and foot, continued westward to seek out the ford of Mevano.

Section by section, squad by squad, Conan's rebels filed down the narrow roads. They camped one more night in the hills and went on. As they descended the final range of foothills, between clumps of conifers they again caught glimpses of the broad Alimane, which sundered Argos from Poitain. True, Argos claimed a tract of land on the northern side of the river – a tract extending to the junction of the Alimane with the Khorotas. But under Vilerus III the Aquilonians had overrun the area and, being the stronger, still retained possession.

As Conan's division reached the flatlands, the Cimmerian ordered his men to speak but little and only in low voices. As far as possible, they were to quiet the jingle of their gear. The wagons halted under heavy stands of trees, and the men pitched camp out of sight of the ford of Mevano. Scouts sent ahead reported no sign of any foe, but they brought back the unwelcome news that the river was in flood, rampant with the springtime melting of the highland snows.

Well before the dawn of a cloud-darkened day, Conan's officers routed the men from their tents. Grumbling, the soldiers bolted an uncooked breakfast and fell into formation. Conan stalked about, snarling curses and threatening those who raised their voices or dropped their weapons. To his apprehensive ears, it seemed as if the clatter could be heard for leagues above the purl of the river. A better-trained force, he thought sourly, would move on cats' paws.

To diminish the noise, commands were passed from captains to men by hand signals instead of by shouts and trumpet calls; and this caused some confusion. One company, signalled to march, cut through the ranks of another. Fisticuffs erupted and noses bled before the officers ended the fracas.

A heavy overcast blanketed road and river as Conan's troops neared the banks of the Alimane. Mounted on his black stallion Fury, Conan drew rein and peered through the curtaining drizzle towards the further bank. Beyond his horse's hooves, the high water, brown with sediment, gurgled past.

Conan signalled to his aide Alaricus, a promising young Aquilonian captain. Alaricus manœuvred his horse close to that of his general.

'How deep, think you?' muttered Conan.

'More than knee-deep, General,' replied Alaricus. 'Perhaps chest-high. Let me put my mount into it to see.'

'Try not to fall into a mudhole,' cautioned Conan.

The young captain urged his bay gelding into the swirling flood. The animal balked, then waded obediently towards the northern shore. By midstream, the murky water was curling over the toes of Alaricus's boots; and when he looked back, Conan beckoned him.

'We shall have to chance it,' growled the Cimmerian when the aide had rejoined him. 'Pass the word for Dio's light horse to make the first crossing and scout the farther woods. Then the foot shall go single file, each man grasping the belt of the man before him. Some of these clodhoppers would drown if they lost their footing whilst weighted with their gear.'

As sunless day paled into the sombre sky, the company of light horse splashed into the stream. Reaching the further bank, Captain Dio waved to indicate that the woods harboured no foe.

Conan had watched intently as the troopers' horses sank into the swirling flume, noting the depth of the water. When it was plain that the river bed shoaled beyond midstream and that the other bank was clear, he signalled the first company of foot to cross. Soon two companies of pikemen and one of archers breasted the flood. Each soldier gripped the man in front, while the archers held aloft their bows to keep them dry.

Conan brought his stallion close to Alaricus, saying: 'Tell the heavy horse to ford the stream, and then start the baggage train across, with Cerco's company of foot to haul them out of mudholes. I'm going out to midstream.'

Fury stumbled into the river, gaskin-deep in the rushing brown water. When the charger flinched and whinnied, as if sensing unseen danger, Conan tightened his grip on the reins and forced the beast through the deepest part of the central channel.

His keen eyes searched the jade-green foliage along the northern shore, where a riot of flowering shrubs, their colours muted by the overcast, surrounded the boles of ancient trees. The road became a dark tunnel amid the new-leaved oaks, which seemed to bear the weight of the leaden sky. Here was ample room for concealment, thought Conan sombrely. The light cavalry still waited, bunched into the small clearing where the road dipped into the river, although they should have searched far into the surrounding woods before the first foot soldiers reached the northern bank. Conan gestured angrily.

'Dio!' he roared from the midstream shallows. If any foe was present, he would long since have observed the crossing, so Conan saw no point in keeping silence. 'Spread out and beat the bushes! Move, damn your soul!'

The three companies of infantry scrambled out on the northern bank, muddy and dripping, while Dio's horsemen broke into squads and pushed into the thickets on either side of the road. An army is at its most vulnerable when fording a stream, this Conan knew; and foreboding swelled in his barbaric heart.

He wheeled his beast about to survey the southern shore. The heavy cavalry was already knee-deep in the stream, and the leading wains of the baggage train were struggling through the flood. A couple had bogged down in the mud of the river bottom; soldiers, heaving on the wheels, man-handled them along.

A sudden cry ripped the heavy air. As Conan swung around, he caught a flicker of movement in the bushes at the junction of road and river. With a short bark of warning, Conan reined his steed, and an arrow meant for him flashed past his breast and, swift as a striking viper, buried itself in the neck of the young officer behind him. As the dying man slumped into the roiling water, Conan spurred his horse forward, bellowing orders. He must, he thought, command the troops in contact with the foe, whether they faced a paltry crossing guard or the full might of Procas's army.

Suddenly Fury reared and staggered beneath the impact of another arrow. With a shriek, the animal fell to its knees, hurling Conan from the saddle. The Cimmerian gulped a swirl of muddy water and struggled to his feet, coughing curses. Another arrow struck his cuirass, glanced off, and tumbled into the torrent. All about him, the stagnant calm of the leaden day hung in tatters. Men howled war cries, screamed in fear and pain, and cursed the very gods above.

Blinking water from his stinging eyes, Conan perceived a triple line of archers and crossbowmen in the blue surcoats of the Border Legion. As one man, they had leaped from the lush foliage to rake the floundering riverbound rebels with a hail of arrows.

The screeching whistle of arrows mingled with the deeper thrum of crossbow bolts. Although the arbalesters could not shoot their cumbersome weapons so fast as the longbowmen, their crossbows had the greater range, and their iron bolts could pierce the stoutest armour. Man after man fell, scream-ing or silent, as the muddy waters closed over their heads and rolled their bodies along the scoured shoals.

Wading shoreward, Conan searched out a trumpeter to call his milling men into battle formations. In the shallows he found one, a tow-headed Gunderman, staring dumbly at the carnage. Growling curses, Conan splashed towards the awestruck lout; but as he sought to seize the fellow's jerkin, the Gunderman doubled up and pitched headfirst into the water, a bolt buried in his vitals. The trumpet fell from his flaccid grip and was tumbled out of reach by the current.

As Conan paused to catch his breath, glaring about like a cornered lion, an augmented clatter from the clearing riveted his attention. Aquilonian cavalry – armoured lancers and swordsmen on sturdy mounts – thundered out of the woods and swept down upon the milling mass of rebel light horse and infantry. The smaller horses of the rebel scouts were brushed aside; the men on foot were ridden down and trampled. In a trice the north bank was cleared of rebels. Then, with clocklike precision, Procas's armoured squadrons opened out into a troop-wide rank of horsemen, which plunged into the water to assail those rebels who struggled in the deeps.

'To me!' roared Conan, brandishing his sword. 'Form squares!'

But now the survivors of the débâcle, who had been swept back into the river by the Aquilonian cavalry, thrashed through the water in panic flight, pushing aside or knocking over comrades who floundered northward. Through the turbulent current pounded Procas's horse amid fountains of spray. Behind the second line, a third line opened out, and then another and another. And from the flanks, Procas's archers continued their barrage of missiles, to which the rebel archers, with unstrung bows, could not reply.

'General!' cried Alaricus. Conan looked around to see the young captain breasting the water towards him. 'Save yourself! They're broken here, but you can rally the men for a stand on the southern bank. Take my horse!'

Conan spat a curse at the fast-approaching line of armoured horsemen. For an instant he hesitated, the thought of rushing among them single-handed, hewing right and left, flickering in his mind. But the idea was banished as soon as it appeared. In an earlier day, Conan might have essayed such a mad attack. Now he was a general, responsible for the lives of other men, and experience had tempered his youthful recklessness with caution. As Alaricus started to dismount, Conan seized the aide's stirrup with his left hand, growling:

'Stay up there lad! Go on, head for the south bank, Crom blast it!'

Alaricus spurred his horse, which struggled towards the Argossean shore. Conan, gripping the stirrup, accompanied him with long, half-leaping strides, amid the retreating mass of rebels, horsed and afoot, all plunging southward in confused and abject flight.

Behind them rode the Aquilonians, spearing and swording the laggards as they fought the flood. Already the muddy waters of the Alimane ran red below the ford of Mevano. Only the fact that the pursuers, too, were hampered by the swirling stream saved Conan's advance units from utter annihilation.

At length the fugitives reached a company of heavy cavalry that had broached the river behind the rebel infantry. The fleeing men pushed between the oncoming horses, yammering their terror. Thus beset, the frightened beasts reared and plunged until their riders, also, joined the retreat. Behind them, mired in the river bottom, teamsters strove to turn their cumbersome supply wagons around or, in despair, abandoned them to leap into the water and splash back towards the southern shore. Coming upon the abandoned vehicles, the Aquilonians butchered the bellowing oxen and pressed on. Sodden corpses, rolled along by the current, wedged together into grisly human log jams. Wagons were overturned; their loads of tent canvas and poles, bundles of spears and sheaves of arrows floated downstream on the relentless flood.

Conan, shouting himself hoarse, struggled out on the south bank, where the remaining companies had awaited their turn to cross. He tried to rally them into defensive formations, but everywhere the rebel host was crumbling into formless clots of fleeing men. Throwing away pikes, shields and helmets, they sought safety, running in all directions out of the shallows and across the flats that bordered the river. All discipline, so painfully inculcated during the preceding months, was lost in the terror of the moment.

A few knots of men stood firm as the Aquilonian cavalry reached them and fought with stubborn ferocity, but they were ridden down and slain or scattered.

Conan found Publius in the crush and seized him by the shoulder, shouting in his ear. Unable to hear his commander above the uproar, the treasurer shrugged helplessly, pointing. At his feet lay the body of Conan's aide, which Publius was shielding from the rough boots of the fleeing soldiery. Alaricus's horse had disappeared.

With an angry bellow, Conan dispersed the crowd around him by striking about with the flat of his blade. Then he hoisted Alaricus to his shoulder and headed southward at a jog trot. The stout Publius ran puffing beside him. Not far behind, the Aquilonian cavalry clambered out of the river to pursue the retreating rebels. They enveloped the line of wains drawn up along the shore, awaiting their turn to breast the flood.

Further inland, some of the teamsters managed to turn their clumsy carts and lashed their oxen into a shambling run back towards the safety of the hills. The road south was black with fleeing men, while hundreds of others darted off across the meadows to lose themselves in the sheltering woods.

Since the day was young and the Aquilonian forces fresh, Conan's division faced annihilation at the hands of their well-mounted pursuers. But here occurred a check – not a great one, but enough to give the fugitives some small advantage. The Aquilonians who had surrounded the supply wagons, instead of pushing on, pulled up to loot the vehicles, despite the shouted commands of their officers. Hearing them, Conan panted:

'Publius! Where's the pay chest?'

'I – know – not,' gasped the treasurer. ' ''Twas in one of the last wains, so perchance it escaped the wreck. I – can – run – no further. Go on, Conan.'

'Don't be a fool!' snarled Conan. 'I need a man who can reckon sums, and my young mealsack here regains his wits.'

As Conan set down his burden, Alaricus opened his eyes

and groaned. Conan, hastily examining him for wounds, found none. The captain, it transpired, had been stunned by a crossbow bolt, which merely grazed his head and dented his helmet. Conan hauled him to his feet.

'I've carried you, my lad,' said the Cimmerian. 'Now 'tis your turn to help me carry our fat friend.'

Soon the three set out again for the safety of the hills, Publius staggering between the other two with an arm about the neck of each. Rain began to fall, gently at first and then in torrents.

The winds of misfortune blew cold on Conan's head that night as he sat in a hollow of the Rabirian Mountains. The day was plainly lost, his men dispersed – those who had survived the battle and the bloody vengeance meted out by the royalist general and his searching parties. In a few hours, it seemed, their very cause had foundered, sunk in the muddy, bloodstained waters of the River Alimane.

Here in a rocky hollow, hidden amid oak and pine, Conan, Publius and five score other rebels waited out the dark and hopeless night. The refugees were a mixed lot: renegade Aquilonian knights, staunch yeomen, armed outlaws and soldiers of fortune. Some were hurt, though few mortally, and many hearts pounded drumbeats of despair.

The legions of Amulius Procas, Conan knew, were sniffing through the hills, bent on slaughtering every survivor. The victorious Aquilonian evidently meant to smash the rebellion for all time by dealing speedy death to every rebel he could catch. Conan grudgingly gave the veteran commander credit for his plan. Had Conan been in Amulius Procas's place, he would have followed much the same course.

Sunk in silent gloom, Conan fretted over the fate of Prospero and Trocero. Prospero was to have feinted at the ford of Nogara, drawing thither the bulk of Procas's troops, so that Conan and Trocero should have only minor contingents of crossing guards to contend with. Instead, Procas's massed warriors had erupted out of concealment when

Conan's van, waist-deep in the Alimane, was at a hopeless disadvantage. Conan wondered how Procas had so cleverly divined the rebels' plans.

Gathered around their fugitive leader, in the lonely dark, huddled men who had been soaked by rain and river. They dared not light a fire lest it become a beacon guiding forces for their destruction. The coughs and sneezes of the fugitives tolled the knell of their hopes. When someone cursed the weather, Conan growled:

'Thank your gods for that rain! Had the day been fair, Procas would have butchered the lot of us. No fire!' he barked at a soldier who tried to strike a light with flint and steel. 'Would you draw Procas's hounds upon us? How many are we? Sound off, but softly. Count them, Publius.'

Men responded 'Here!' 'Here!' while Publius kept track with his fingers. When the last 'Here!' had been heard, he said:

'One hundred thirteen, General, not counting ourselves.'

Conan grunted. Brightly though the lust for revenge burned in his barbarian heart, it seemed impossible that such a paltry number could form the nucleus of another army. While he put up a bold front before his rebel remnant, the vulture of despondency clawed at his weary flesh.

He set out sentries, and during the night exhausted men, guided by these sentinels, stumbled into the hollow in ones and twos and threes. Towards midnight came Dextheus, the priest of Mitra, limping along on an improvised crutch, leaning heavily on the arm of the sentry who guided him and wincing with the pain of a wrenched ankle.

Now there were nearly twice a hundred fugitives, some gravely wounded, gathered in the hollow. The Mitraist priest, despite the pain of his own injury, set to work to tend the wounded, drawing arrows from limbs and bandaging wounds for hours, until Conan brusquely commanded him to rest.

The camp was rude, its comforts primitive; and, Conan knew, the rebels had little chance of seeing another nightfall. But at least they were alive, most still bore arms, and many could put up a savage fight if Procas should discover their hiding place. And so, at last, Conan slept.

Dawn mounted a sky where clouds were breaking up and dwindling, leaving a clear blue vault. Conan was awakened by the subdued chatter of many armed men. The newcomers were Prospero and his diversionary detachment, five hundred strong.

'Prospero!' cried Conan, struggling to his feet to clasp his friend in a mighty embrace. Then he led the officer aside and spoke in a low voice, lest ill tidings should further depress the spirits of the men. 'Thank Mitra! How went your day? How did you find us? What of Trocero?'

'One at a time, General,' said Prospero, catching his breath. 'We found naught but a few crossing guards at Nogara, and they fled before us. For a whole day, we marched in circles, blew trumpets and beat drums, but no royalists could we draw to the ford. Thinking this strange, I sent a galloper downstream to Tunais. He reported a hard fight there, with Trocero's division in retreat. Then a fugitive from your command fell in with us and spoke of your disaster. So, not wishing my small force to be caught between the millstones of two enemy divisions, I fell back into the uplands. There, other runagates told us of the direction they had seen you take. Now, what of you?'

Conan clenched his teeth to stifle his self-reproach. 'I played the fool this time, Prospero, and led us into Procas's jaws. I should have waited until Dio had probed the forest ere starting my lads across. It's well that Dio fell at the first onslaught – had he not, I'd have made him wish he had. He and his men milled around like sheep for a snailish time ere pushing out to beat the undergrowth. But still, I was at fault to let impatience sway me. Procas had watchers in the trees, to signal the attack. Now all is lost.'

'Not so, Conan,' said Prospero. 'As you are wont to say, naught is hopeless until the last man chews the dust or knuckles under; and in every war the gods throw boons and banes to either side. Let us fall back to the Plain of Pallos and our base camp. We may join Trocero along the way. We are now several hundred strong, and we shall count to thousands when we sweep up the other stragglers. A hundred gullies in these hills must shelter groups like ours.'

'Procas far outnumbers us,' said Conan sombrely, 'and his well-found forces carry high spirits from their victories. What can a few thousand, downcast by defeat, achieve against them? Besides, he will have seized the passes through the Rabirians, or at least the main pass at Saxula.'

'Doubtless,' said Prospero, 'but Procas's troops are scattered wide, searching for fugitives. Our hungry pride of lions could one by one devour his packs of bloodhounds. In sooth, we came upon one such on our way hither – a squad of light horse – and slew the lot. Come, General! You of all men are the indomitable one – the man who never quits. You've built a band of brigands into an army and shaken thrones ere now; you can do the same again. So be of good cheer!'

Conan took a deep breath and squared his massive shoulders. 'You're right, by Crom! I'll mewl no longer like a starving beldame. We've lost one engagement, but our cause remains whilst there be two of us to stand back to back and fight for it. And we have this, at least.'

He reached into the shadows and drew from a crevice in the rocks the Lion banner, the symbol of the rebellion. His standard bearer, though mortally wounded, had borne it to the hollow in the hills. After the man had succumbed, Conan had rolled up the banner and thrust it out of sight. Now he unfurled it in the pale light of dawn.

'It's little enough to salvage from the rout of an army,' he rumbled, 'but thrones have been won with less.' And Conan smiled a grim, determined smile.

V

The Purple Lotus

The smiling day revealed that Fate had not entirely forsaken the army of the rebellion. For the night had been heavily overcast, and in the gloom the weary warriors of Amulius Procas had failed to root out many scattered pockets of survivors, like that which Conan had gathered around him. Thus, as the morning sun rolled back its blanket of clouds, bands of heartsore rebels, who had either eluded the search parties or routed those they encountered, began to filter back across the Rabirian range.

Night was nigh when Conan and his remnant approached the pass of Saxula. Conan dispatched men ahead to scout, since he was convinced he would have to fight his way through. He snorted with surprise when the scouts reported back that there was no evidence of the Border Legion anywhere near the pass. There were signs – the ashes of campfires and other debris – that a force of Procas's men had camped in the pass, but they were nowhere to be seen.

'Crom! What means this?' Conan mused, staring up at the great notch in the ridge. 'Unless Procas has sent his men on, deeper into Argos.'

'I think not,' said Publius. 'That would mean open war with Milo. More likely, he ordered his men back across the Alimane before the court at Messantia could hear of his incursion. Then, if King Milo protests, Procas can aver that not one Aquilonian soldier remains on Argossean soil.'

'Let's hope you are right,' said Conan. 'Forward, men!'

By the next midday, Conan's band had gathered up several full companies that had fled unscathed from the ambush at Mevano. But the rebels' greatest prize was Count Trocero himself, camped on a hilltop with two hundred horse and foot. Having built a rude palisade, the Count of Poitain was prepared to hold his little fort against Procas and all his iron legions. Trocero emotionally embraced Conan and Prospero.

'Thank Mitra you live!' he cried. 'I heard that you had fallen to an arrow and that your division fled southward like wintering wildfowl.'

'You hear many things about a battle, perhaps one tenth of them true,' said Conan. He told the tale of the ambush at Mevano and asked: 'How fared you at Tunais?'

'Procas smashed us as badly as he shattered you. I believe that he himself commanded. He laid his ambush on the south bank of the river and assailed us from both sides as we prepared to cross. I had not thought that he would dare so grossly to violate Argossean territory.'

'Amulius Procas is nobody's fool,' said Conan, 'nor does he scruple to snatch at a long chance when he must. But how came you hither? Through Saxula Pass?'

'Nay. When we approached it, a strong force of Procas's men were there encamped. Luckily, one of my horsemen, a smuggler by trade, knew a narrow, little-used opening through which he led us. It was a dizzy climb, but we got through with the loss of but two beasts. Now, say you that Saxula Pass is open?'

'It was last night, at least.' said Conan. He looked around. 'Let's go on, posthaste, back to our base camp on the Plain of Pallos. My men together with yours make above a thousand fighters.'

'A thousand scarce an army makes,' grumbled Publius. ' 'Tis but a remnant of the ten thousand who marched northward with us.'

'It's a beginning,' said Conan, whose gloom of the night before had vanished with the light of day. 'I can recall when our whole enterprise numbered only five stout hearts.'

As the remnant of the rebels marched, more bands that had escaped the slaughter joined the host, and individual survivors and small groups came straggling in. Conan kept glancing back with apprehension, expecting at any moment to see Procas's whole Border Legion pour down the Rabirian Hills in hot pursuit. But Publius thought differently.

'Look you, General,' he said. 'King Milo has not yet betrayed us or turned against us, or surely he would have come pounding at our rear whilst Procas engaged us in the van. Methinks not even the mad King of Aquilonia dare risk a full and open war with the sovereign state of Argos; the Argosseans are a hardy lot. Amulius Procas knows his politics; he would not have so long survived in Numedides's service had he rashly affronted neighbouring kingdoms. Once we regain our base camp and shore up our barricades, we should be safe for the moment. The reserve supplies and the camp followers await us.'

Conan scowled. 'Until Numedides bribes or bullies Milo into turning his hand against us.'

In a sense, Conan was right. For even at that hour, the agents of Aquilonia were closeted with King Milo and his councilmen. Chief among these agents was Quesado the Zingaran, who had reached Messantia with his party by a long, hard ride from Tarantia, swinging wide of the embattled armies.

Quesado, now resplendent in black velvet with boots of fine red Kordavan leather, had changed; and the change was not to his employer's advantage. Hearing of the spy's exploits in the service of Vibius Latro, a delighted King Numedides had insisted on promoting Quesado to the diplomatic corps. This proved a mistake.

The Zingaran had been an excellent spy, long trained to affect an unassuming, inconspicuous air. Now suddenly raised in pay and prestige, he let his façade of humility crumble, and the pompous pride and hauteur of a would-be Zingaran gentleman began to show through the gaps. Looking down his beak of a nose, he endeavoured by thinly veiled threats to persuade King Milo and his councillors that it were wiser to court the favour of the King of Aquilonia than to support his raggle-taggle foes.

'My lord King and gentlemen,' said Quesado in a sharp, schoolmasterish voice, 'surely you know that, if you choose to be no friend of my master, you must be counted amongst his enemies. And the longer you permit your realm to shelter our rebellious foes, the more you will be tainted with the poison of treason against my sovereign lord, the mighty King of Aquilonia.'

King Milo's broad face flushed with anger, and he sat up sharply. A heavy-set man of middle years, whose luxuriant grey beard overspread his chest, Milo gave the impression of stolid taciturnity, more like some honest peasant than the ruler of a rich and sophisticated realm. Slow to make up his mind, he could be exceedingly stubborn once he had reached his decision. Glaring at Quesado, he snapped:

'Argos is a free and sovereign state, sirrah! We have never been and, Mitra willing, never shall be subject to the King of Aquilonia. Treason means a misdeed of a subject against his overlord. Do you claim that fat Numedides is overlord of Argos?'

Quesado began to perspire; his bony forehead gleamed damply in the soft light that streamed in ribbons of azure, vert and scarlet through the stained-glass windows of the council chamber.

'Such was not my intention, Your Majesty,' he hastily apologized. More humbly, he pleaded: 'But with all respect, sire, I must point out that my master can hardly overlook assistance given by a neighbouring brother monarch to rebels against his divinely established Ruby Throne.'

'We have given them no help,' said Milo, glowering. 'Your spies will have apprized you that their remnants are encamped upon the Plain of Pallos and, lacking supplies from Messantia, are desperately scouring the countryside for food. Their famed Bossonian archers employ their skill in pursuing ducks and deer. You say your General Procas's victory was decisive? What, then, has mighty Aquilonia to fear from a gaggle of fugitives, reduced by starvation to mere banditry? We are told they have but a tithe of their original strength and that desertions further reduce their numbers day by day.'

'True, my lord King,' said Quesado, who had recovered his poise. 'But, by the same token, what has cultured Argos to gain by sheltering such a band? Unable to assail their rightful ruler, they must needs maintain themselves by depredations against your own loyal subjects.'

Scowling, Milo lapsed into silence, for he had no convincing answer to Quesado's argument. He could hardly say that he had given his word to an old friend, Count Trocero, to let the rebels use his land as a base for operations against a neighbouring king. Moreover, he resented the Aquilonian envoy's efforts to rush him into a decision. He liked to make up his own mind in his own time, without hectoring.

Lumbering to his feet, the king curtly adjourned the session: 'We will consider the requests of our brother monarch, Ambassador Quesado. Our gentlemen shall inform you of our decision at our pleasure. You have our leave to withdraw.'

Lips curled in a false smile, Quesado bowed his way out, but venom ate at his heart. Fortune had favoured the rebellious Cimmerian this time, he thought, but the next throw of the dice might have a different outcome. For though he knew it not, Conan nursed a viper in his bosom.

The Army of the Lion was in no wise so enfeebled or reduced to famine as Milo and Quesado believed. Now numbering over fifteen hundred, it daily rebuilt its strength and gathered supplies. The lean horses grazed on the long grass of the plain; the women camp followers, who had been left at the base camp when the army marched northward, nursed the wounded. Much of the baggage train had been salvaged, and ragged survivors continued to limp and straggle in, to swell the thin but resolute ranks of the rebellion. The forests whispered to the footfalls of hunters and rang to the axes of woodcutters, while in the camp, fletchers whittled spear and arrow shafts, and the anvils of blacksmiths clanged with the beat of hammers on point and blade.

Most encouraging was the tale that the rear guard, a

thousand strong under the Aquilonian Baron Groder, had escaped the débâcle at Tunais and was wandering in the mountains to the east. To investigate, Conan sent Prospero with a troop of light horse to search for their lost comrades and guide them to the base. Dexitheus prayed to Mitra that this rumour might prove true, for the addition of Groder's force would nearly double their strength. Kingdoms had fallen ere this to fewer than three thousand determined warriors.

A full moon glared down upon the Plain of Pallos like the yellow eye of an angry god. A chill, uneasy wind rustled through the tall meadow grasses and plucked with ghostly fingers at the cloaks of sentries, who stood watch about the rebel camp.

In his candle-lit tent, Conan sat late over a flagon of ale, listening to his officers. Some, still downcast by their recent defeat, were reluctant to contemplate further conflicts at this time. Others, avid for revenge, urged an early assault, even with their present diminished might.

'Look you, General,' said Count Trocero. 'Amulius Procas will never expect an attack so soon upon the heels of our disaster, so we shall take him by surprise. Once across the Alimane, we shall be joined by our Poitanian friends, who only await our coming to raise the province.'

Conan's savage soul incited him to heed his friend's advice. To strike across the border now, at the very ebb of their fortunes, would wrest victory from defeat with a vengeance. He urgently needed a vigorous sally to mend the men's morale. Already some were drifting away, deserting what they viewed as a hopeless cause. Unless he could shore up the dykes of loyalty with hopes of triumph, the leakage of the disaffected would soon become a flood, leaching his army away to nothing.

Yet the mighty Cimmerian had, during his years of campaigning, grown wise in the ways of war. Experience cautioned him to rein in his eagerness, rather than commit his remaining strength – at least until Prospero returned with word of

Baron Groder and his force. Once Conan knew he could count upon this powerful reinforcement, he could then determine whether the moment for assault was at hand.

Dismissing his commanders, Conan sought the warm arms and soft breasts of Alcina. The golden dancing girl had entranced him with her wily ways of assuaging his passions; but this night she laughingly eluded his embrace, to proffer a goblet of wine.

' 'Tis time, my lord, that you enjoyed a gentleman's drink, instead of swilling bitter beer like any peasant,' she said. 'I brought a flask of fine wine from Messantia for your especial pleasure.'

'Crom and Mitra, girl, I've drunk enough this night! I thirst now for the wine of your lips, not for the pressings of the grape.'

'It is but a gentle stimulant, lord, to augment your desires – and my enjoyment of them,' she wheedled. Standing in the candlelight in a length of sheer saffron silk, which did little to hide the lush lines of her body, she smiled seductively and thrust the goblet towards him, saying: 'It contains spices from my homeland to rouse your senses. Will you not drink it, my lord, to please me?'

Looking eagerly upon the moon-pale oval of her face, Conan said: 'I need no rousing when I smell the perfume of your hair. But give it to me; I'll drink to this night's delights.'

He drank the wine in three great gulps, ignoring the faintly acrid taste of the spices, and slammed the goblet down. Then he reached for the delectable girl, whose wide-set eyes were fixed upon him.

But, when he sought to seize her in his arms, the tent reeled crazily about him, and a searing pain bloomed in his vitals. He snatched at the tent pole, missed, and fell heavily.

Alcina leaned over his supine body. In his blurring vision, her features melted into a mist, through which her green eyes burned like incandescent emeralds.

'Crom's blood, wench!' Conan gasped. 'You've poisoned me!'

He struggled to rise, but it seemed to the Cimmerian that his body had turned to lead. Although the veins in his temples throbbed, his face purpled with effort, and his thews stood out along his limbs like ship's cables, he could not regain his feet. He fell back, gulping air. Then his vision dimmed until he seemed to drift from the lamplit interior of the tent into a trancelike waking dream. He could neither speak nor stir.

'Conan!' the girl murmured, bending over him, but he made no reply. In a silken whisper, she said: 'So much for you, barbarian pig! And soon your wretched remnant of an army will follow you back to the hells whence you and they once crawled!'

Calmly seating herself, she drew forth the amulet she bore between her breasts. A glance at the time candle on a taboret showed that half an hour must yet elapse before she could commune with her master. In sphinxlike silence she sat, unmoving, until the time approached. Then she focused her mind upon the obsidian fragment.

In far-off Tarantia, Thulandra Thuu, gazing into his magical mirror, gave a dry chuckle as he observed the quiescent form of the giant Cimmerian. Rising, he replaced the mirror in its cabinet, roused his servant, and sent him with a message to the king.

Hsiao found Numedides, unclothed, enjoying a massage by four handsome naked girls. Keeping his modest eyes fixed upon the marble floor, Hsiao bowed low and said:

'My master respectfully informs Your Majesty that the bandit rebel Conan is slain in Argos by my master's other-worldly powers.'

With a grunt, Numedides sat up, pushing the girls away. 'Eh? Dead, you say?'

'Aye, my lord King.'

'Excellent news, excellent news.' With a loud guffaw, Numedides slapped his bare thigh. 'When I become a – but enough of that. What else?'

'My master asks your permission to send a message to General Amulius Procas, informing him of this event and authorising him to cross into Argos, to scatter the rebel remnants ere they can choose another leader.'

Numedides waved the Khitan away. 'Begone, yellow dog, and tell your master to do as he thinks best. Now let us continue, girls.'

Thus, later that night, a courier set out along the far-flung road to General Procas's headquarters on the Argossean frontier. The message, which bore the seal of King Numedides, would in less than a fortnight loose the fury of the Border Legion upon the leaderless men who followed the Lion banner.

In Conan's tent, Alcina opened her travelling chest and dug out a page's costume, into which she changed. Under the garments in the chest lay a small copper casket, which she opened by twisting the silver dragon that bestrode the lid. The casket contained a choice assortment of rings, bracelets, necklaces, ear-rings and other gem-encrusted finery. Alcina burrowed into the jewellery until she found a small oblong of copper, inscribed in Argossean. This token – a forgery provided by Quesado – entitled the bearer to change horses at the royal post stations. She made a quick selection of the jewellery, tucking the better pieces into her girdle, and filled the small purse depending from her belt with coins of gold and silver.

Then she extinguished the candle and boldly left the darkened tent. Demurely she addressed the sentry: 'The general sleeps; but he has asked me to bear an urgent message to the court of Argos. Will you kindly order the grooms to saddle a horse, forthwith, and fetch it hither?'

The sentry called the corporal of the guard, who sent a man to comply with Alcina's request, while the girl waited silently at the entrance to the tent. The soldiers, who were used to the comings and goings of the general's mistress and admired her splendid figure and easy ways, hastened to do her bidding.

When the horse was brought, she mounted swiftly and followed the sentry assigned to her beyond the limits of the camp. Then, at a spanking trot, she vanished into the moonlit distance.

Four days later, Alcina arrived in Messantia. She hastened to Quesado's hideaway, where she found the spy's replacement, Fadius the Kothian, feeding Quesado's carrier pigeons. She asked:

'Pray, where is Quesado?'

'Have you not heard?' replied Fadius. 'He's an ambassador now, too proud to spare time for the likes of us. He's been here but once since he arrived on his embassy.'

'Well, grandee or no grandee, I must see him at once. I bear news of the greatest import.'

Grumbling, Fadius led Alcina to the hostelry in Messantia where the Aquilonians lodged. Quesado's servant was pulling off his master's boots and preparing him for bed when Alcina and Fadius burst in unannounced.

'Damme!' cried Quesado. 'What sort of ill-bred rabble are you, to intrude on a gentleman retiring for the night?'

'You know well enough who we are,' said Alcina. 'I came to tell you Conan is dead.'

Quesado paused with his mouth open, then closed it slowly. 'Well!' he said at last. 'That casts a different light on many matters. Pull on my boots again, Narses. I must go to the palace forthwith. What has befallen, Mistress Alcina?'

A little time later, Quesado presented himself at the palace with a peremptory demand to see the king. The Zingaran intended to urge an instant attack on Conan's army by the forces of Argos. He felt sure that the rebels, demoralized by the fall of their leader, would crumble before any vigorous assault.

Fate, however, ordained that events should march to a different tune. Roused from slumber, King Milo flew into a rage at Quesado's insolence in demanding a midnight audience.

'His Majesty,' reported the head page to Quesado,

71

'commands that you depart instanter and return at a more seemly time. He suggests an hour before noon tomorrow.'

Quesado flushed with the anger of frustration. Looking down his nose, he said: 'My good man, you do not seem to realise who and what I am.'

The page laughed, matching Quesado's impudence with his own. 'Aye, sir, we all know who you are – and what you were.' Derisive grins spread to the faces of the guards flanking the page, who continued: 'Now pray depart hence, and speedily, on pain of my sovereign lord's displeasure!'

'You shall rue those words, varlet!' snarled Quesado, turning away. He tramped the cobbled streets to his former headquarters on the waterfront, where he found Fadius and Alcina awaiting him. There he prepared a furious dispatch to the King of Aquilonia, telling of Milo's rebuff, and sent it on its way wired to the leg of a pigeon.

In a few days, the former spy's report reached Vibius Latro, who brought it to his king's attention. Numedides, seldom able to restrain his passions under the easiest of circumstances, read of the recalcitrance of the King of Argos towards his mighty neighbour and sent another courier posthaste to General Amulius Procas. This dispatch did more than authorise an incursion into Argos, as had the previous message. In exigent terms, it commanded the general at once to attack across the borders of Argos, with whatever force he needed, to stamp out the last embers of the rebellion.

Procas, a tough and canny old campaigner, winced at the royal command. On the night that followed his victorious battles on the Alimane, he had quickly withdrawn from Argossean territory the detachments he had sent across the river to harry the fleeing rebels. Those incursions could be excused on grounds of hot pursuit. But now, if he mounted a new invasion, the open violation of the border would almost certainly turn King Milo's sympathies from cautious neutrality into open hostility to the royal Aquilonian cause.

But the royal command admitted of no argument or

refusal. If he wished his head to continue to ride his shoulders, Procas must attack, although every instinct in his soldierly bosom cried out against this hasty, ill-timed instruction.

Procas delayed his advance for several days, hoping that the king, on second thoughts, would countermand his order. But no communication came, and Procas dared wait no longer. And so, on a bright spring morning, Amulius Procas crossed the Alimane in force. The river, which had subsided somewhat from its flood, offered no obstacle to his squadrons of glittering, panoplied knights, stolid mailed spearmen and leather-coated archers. They splashed across and marched implacably up the winding road that led to Saxula Pass through the Rabirian range, and thence to the rebel camp on the Plain of Pallos.

Not until the morning after Alcina's departure did Conan's officers learn of the fall of their leader. They gathered round him, laid him on his bed, and searched him for wounds. Dexitheus, still limping on a walking stick, sniffed at the dregs in the goblet from which Conan had drunk Alcina's potion.

'That drink,' he said, 'was laced with the juice of the purple lotus of Stygia. By rights, our general should be as dead as King Tuthamon; yet he lives, albeit no more than a living corpse with open eyes.'

Publius flicked his fingers as he did mental sums and mused: 'Perchance the poisoner used only so much of the drug as would suffice to slay an ordinary man, unmindful of Conan's great size and strength.'

' 'Twas that green-eyed witch!' cried Trocero. 'I've never trusted her, and her disappearance last night proclaims her guilt. Were she in my power, I'd burn her at the stake!'

Dexitheus turned on the count. 'Green eyes, quotha? A woman with green eyes?'

'Aye, as green as emeralds. But what of it? Surely you know Conan's concubine, the fair Alcina.'

Dexitheus shook his head with a frown of foreboding. 'I heard that our general had taken a dancing girl from the wineshops of Argos,' he murmured, 'but I try to ignore such whoredoms among my sons, and Conan tactfully kept her out of my sight. Woe unto our cause! For the lord Mitra warned me in a dream to beware a green-eyed shadow hovering near our leader, although I knew not that the evil one already walked amongst us. Woe unto me, who failed to confide the warning to my comrades!'

'Enough of this,' said Publius. 'Conan lives, and we can thank our gods that our fair poisoner is no arithmetician. Let none but his squires attend him or even enter the tent. We must tell the men that he is ill of a minor tisick, whilst we continue to rebuild our force. If he recovers, he recovers; but meanwhile you must take command, Trocero.'

The Poitanian count nodded sombrely. 'I'll do what I can, since I am second in command. You, Publius, must mend the nets of your spy system, so that we shall have warning of Procas's moves. It's time for morning roll call, so I must be off. I'll drill the lads as hard as Conan ever drilled them, aye and more!'

By the time Procas began his invasion, the Lions again had their watching eyes and listening ears abroad. Reports of the strength of the invaders reached the leaders of the rebel army, who had gathered in Conan's tent. Trocero, wearing the silvery badge of age and the lines of weariness but self-assured withal, asked Publius:

'What know we of the numbers of the foe?'

Publius bent his head to work sums on his waxen tablets. When he raised his eyes, his expression showed alarm. 'Thrice our strength and more,' he said heavily. 'This is a black day, my friends. We can do little save make a final stand.'

'Be of good cheer!' said the count, slapping the stout treasurer on the back. 'You'd never make a general, Publius; you'd assure the soldiers they were beaten before the fray began.' He turned to Dexitheus. 'How does our patient?'

'He regains some slight awareness, but as yet he cannot

74

move. I now think he will live, praise Mitra.'

'Well, if he cannot sit a horse when the battle trumpet blows, I must sit it for him. Have we any word of Prospero?'

Publius and Dexitheus shook their heads. Trocero shrugged, saying: 'Then we must make do with what we have. The foe will close within striking distance on the morrow, and we must needs decide whether to fight or flee.'

Down from the mountains streamed the armoured cavalry and infantry of the Border Legion. A swirl of galloping scouts preceded them, and in their midst rode General Amulius Procas in his chariot. Drawn up to confront them, the rebels formed their battle lines in the midst of the plain.

The still air offered no respite from the myriad fears and silent prayers of the waiting men. The broad front of the superior Aquilonian force allowed Count Trocero no opportunity for clever flanking or enveloping moves. Yet, to retreat now would mean the instant dissolution of the rebel force. The count knew there could be no shrewdly timed withdrawal, with rear-guard actions to delay pursuit. Such a fighting retreat was only for well-trained, self-confident troops. These men, discouraged by their fortune on the Alimane, would simply flee, every man for himself, while the Aquilonian light horse rode down the fugitives, slaying and slaying until nightfall sheltered the survivors beneath its dragon wings.

Trocero, scanning the oncoming host from his command post on a hillock, presently signalled his groom to fetch his charger. He adjusted a strap on his armour and heaved himself into the saddle. To the few hundred horsemen who gathered around him, he said:

'You know our plan, my friends. 'Tis a slim chance, but our only one.'

For Trocero had decided that their only hope lay in a suicidal charge into the Aquilonian array, in a mad effort to reach Amulius Procas himself. He knew that the enemy commander, a stout man of middle years slowed by ancient wounds, found riding hard on his ageing joints and preferred to travel by chariot. He knew, too, that the general's charioteer would have difficulty in manœuvring the clumsy vehicle in the press of battle. Thus, if the rebel horse could by some miracle reach and slay the Aquilonian general, his troops might falter and break.

The outlook, as Trocero had said, was black, but the plan was the best he could devise. Meanwhile he strove to give his subordinates no sign of his discomfiture. He laughed and joked as if he faced certain victory instead of a forlorn attempt to vanquish thrice their number of the world's best soldiery.

Once again, Destiny intervened on the side of the rebels, in the royal person of Milo, King of Argos. Even before the Aquilonian invasion began, an Argossean spy, killing three horses in his haste to reach Messantia, brought word to the court of Numedides's command to violate the territory of Argos. Thus King Milo learned of the planned attack as soon as did the rebel commanders. Already affronted by the arrogance of Ambassador Quesado, the usually even-tempered Milo flew into a rage. At once he commanded the nearest division of his army to speed north on forced marches to intercept the invasion.

In a calmer moment, Milo might have temporised. Since he did not think that Numedides meant to seize a portion of his land, as the late King Vilerus had done, he had sound reasons for delaying any irrevocable action. But, by the time his temper had cooled, his troops were already on the march northward, and with his usual stubbornness the king refused to change his decision.

Amulius Procas had halted his army and was meticulously ordering his troops for an assault when a breathless scout galloped up to his chariot.

'General!' he cried, gasping for breath. 'A great cloud of dust is rising from the southern road; it is as if another army approached!'

Procas made the scout repeat his message. Then, blueing

the air with curses, he tugged off his helmet and hurled it with a clang to the floor of his chariot. It was as he had feared; King Milo had got wind of the invasion and was sending troops to block it. To his aides he barked:

'Tell the men to stand at ease, and see that they have water. Order the scouts to swing around the rebel army and probe to southward, to learn the numbers and composition of the approaching force. Pitch a tent, and call my high officers to a conference.'

When, an hour later, the scouts reported that a thousand cavalry were on the march, Amulius Procas found himself caught on the horns of a dilemma. Without explicit orders from his king, he dared not provoke Argos into open warfare. Neither did he dare disobey a direct command from Numedides without some overriding reason.

True, Procas's army could doubtless crush the rebels and chase Milo's cavalry back to Messantia. But such an action would presage a major war, for which Aquilonia was ill-prepared. While his country was the larger and more populous kingdom, her king was, at least, eccentric; and his rule had gravely weakened mighty Aquilonia. The Argosseans, moreover, fighting with righteous indignation an invader on their native soil, might with the aid of a small rebel force, like that assembled beneath the Lion banner, tip the scales against Procas's homeland.

Neither could Procas retreat. Since his troops outnumbered the combined rebel and Argossean forces, King Numedides might readily read his withdrawal as an act of cowardice or treachery and shorten him by a head for his disobedience.

As the sun rode down the western sky, Procas, deep in discussion with his officers, still delayed his decision. At last he said:

' 'Tis too late to start an action this day. We shall withdraw to northward, where we have left the baggage train, and set up a fortified camp. Send a man to order the engineers to begin digging.'

Trocero, narrowly watching the royalists from his rise, had long since dismounted. Beside him stood Publius, munching on a fowl's leg. At last the treasurer said:

'What in Mitra's name is Procas doing? He had us where he wanted us, and now he pulls back and pitches camp. Is he mad? For aught he knows, we might slip away in the coming night, or steal past him to enter Aquilonia.'

Trocero shrugged. 'Belike the report we had, of Argosseans approaching, has something to do with his actions. It remains to be seen whether these Argossean horsemen mean to help or harm us. We could be caught between the two forces and ground to powder, unless Procas counts on the Argosseans to do his dirty work for him.'

Even as the count spoke, hoofbeats summoned his glance southward across the plain. Soon a small party of mounted men cantered up the rise – a group of Argosseans, guided in by a rebel cavalryman. Two of these new arrivals dismounted with a clank of armour and strode forward. One was tall, lean, and leathery of visage, with the look of a professional soldier. His companion was younger and short of stature, with a wide-cheeked, snub-nosed face and bright, interested eyes. He wore a gilded cuirass and a purple cloak edged with scarlet, and purple-and-scarlet were the plumes that danced on the crest of his helm.

The lean veteran spoke first: 'Hail, Count Trocero! I am Arcadio, senior captain of the Royal Guard, at your service, sir. May I present Prince Cassio of Argos, heir apparent to the throne? We desire a council with your general, Conan the Cimmerian.'

Nodding to the officer and making a slight bow to the Prince of Argos, Trocero said: 'I remember you well, Prince Cassio, as a mischievous child and a harum-scarum youth. As for General Conan, I regret to say he is indisposed. But you may state the purpose of your visit to me as second-in-command.'

'Our purpose, Count Trocero,' said the prince, 'is to thwart this Aquilonian violation of our territorial integrity. To that endeavour, my royal father has sent me hither with such force as could readily be mustered. I assume my officers and I may consider you and your followers as allies?'

Trocero smiled. 'Thrice welcome, Prince Cassio! From your aspect, you have had a long and dusty ride. Will you and Captain Arcadio come to our command tent for refreshment, while your escort take their ease? Our wine has long since gone, but we still have ale.'

On the way back to the tent, Trocero spoke privately to Publius: 'This explains Procas's withdrawal when he all but had us in his jaws. He dare not attack for fear of starting an unauthorised war with Argos, and he dare not retreat lest he be branded a poltroon. So he camps where he is, awaiting –'

'Trocero!' A deep roar came from within the tent. 'Who is it you are talking to, besides Publius? Fetch him in!'

'That's General Conan,' said Trocero, dissembling his startlement. 'Will you step inside, gentlemen?'

They found Conan, in shirt and short breeks, propped up on his bunk. Under the ministrations of Dexitheus, he had recovered full consciousness, his mighty frame having thrown off the worst effects of a draught that would have doomed an ordinary man. While he could think and speak, he could do little else; for the residue of the poison still chained his brawny limbs. Unable to rise without help, he chafed at his confinement.

'Gods and devils!' he fumed. 'Could I but stand and lift a sword, I'd show Procas how to cut and thrust! And who are these Argosseans?'

Trocero introduced Prince Cassio and Captain Arcadio and recounted Procas's latest move. Conan snarled:

'This I will see for myself. Squires! Raise me to my feet. Procas may be shamming a withdrawal, the better to surprise us by a night attack.'

With an arm around the neck of each squire, Conan tottered to the entrance. The sun, impaled upon the peaks of the Rabirian Hills to westward, spilled dark shadows down the mountainsides. In the middle distance, the departing rays struck scarlet sparks from the armour of the Aquilonians as they laboured to set up a camp. The tap of mallets on tent pegs came softly through the evening air.

'Will Procas seek a parley, think you?' asked Conan. The others shrugged.

'He has sent no message yet; he may never do so,' said Trocero. 'We must wait and see.'

'We've waited all day,' growled Conan, 'keeping our lads standing in harness in the sun. I, for one, would that something happened – anything, to end this dawdling.'

'Methinks our general is about to have his wish,' murmured Dexitheus, shading his eyes with his hand as he peered at the distant royalist camp. The other stared at him.

'What now, sir priest?' said Conan.

'Behold!' said Dexitheus, pointing.

'Ishtar!' breathed Captain Arcadio. 'Fry my guts if they're not running away!'

And so they were; if not running, they were at least beginning an orderly retreat. Trumpets sounded, thin and far-away. Instead of continuing to strengthen the fortification of their camp, the men of the Border Legion, antlike in the distance, were striking the tents they had just set up, loading the supply wagons, and streaming out, company by company, towards the pass in the Rabirian Hills. Conan and his comrades looked at one another in perplexity.

The cause of this withdrawal soon transpired. Marching briskly from the east, a fourth host came around the slope of a hill. More than fifteen hundred strong, as Trocero estimated them, the newcomers deployed and advanced on a broad front, ready for battle.

A rebel scout, lashing his horse up the slope, threw himself off his mount, saluted Conan, and gasped: 'My lord general, they fly the leopards of Poitain and the arms of Baron Groder of Aquilonia!'

'Crom and Mitra!' whispered Conan. Then his face cleared and his laughter echoed among the hills. For it was indeed

Prospero with the rebel force that he had searched for in the east.

'No wonder Procas runs!' said Trocero. 'Now that we outnumber him, he can do so without arousing his sovereign's ire. He'll tell Numedides that three armies would have surrounded him at once and overwhelmed him.'

'General Conan,' said Dexitheus, 'you must return to your bed to rest. We cannot afford to have you suffer a relapse.'

As the squires lowered Conan to his pallet, the Cimmerian whispered: 'Prospero, Prospero! For this I will make you a knight of the throne, if ever Aquilonia be mine!'

In Fadius's dingy room in Messantia, Alcina sat alone, holding her obsidian amulet before her and watching the alternate black-and-white bands of the time candle. Fadius was out prowling the nighted streets of the city; Alcina had brusquely ordered him forth so that she could privately commune with her master.

The flickering flame sank lower as the candle burned down through one of the black stripes in the wax. As the last of the sable band dissolved into molten wax and the flame wavered above a white band, the witch-dancer raised her talisman and focused her thoughts. Faintly, like words spoken in a dream, there came into her receptive mind the dry tones of Thulandra Thuu; while before her, barely visible in the dim-lit chamber, appeared a vision of the sorcerer himself, seated in his iron chair.

Thulandra Thuu's speech rustled so softly through Alcina's mind that it demanded rapt attention, together with a constant surveillance of the lips and the gestures of the vision, to grasp the magician's message: 'You have done well, my daughter. Has aught befallen in Messantia?'

She shook her head, and the ghostly whisper continued: 'Then I have another task for you. With the morn's first light, you shall don your page's garb, take horse, and follow the road north –'

Alcina gave a small cry of dismay. 'Must I wear those

ugly rags and plunge again into the wilderness, with ants and beetles for bedmates? I beg you, Master, let me stay here and be a woman yet a while!'

The sorcerer raised a sardonic eyebrow. 'You prefer the fleshpots of Messantia?' he responded.

She nodded vigorously.

'That cannot be, alas. Your duties there are finished, and I need you to watch the Border Legion and its general. If you find the going rough, bear in mind the future glories I have promised you.

'The troops dispatched by the Argossean King should now have reached the Plain of Pallos. Ere the sun rises twice again, Amulius Procas will in all likelihood have concluded a retreat back across the Alimane into Poitain. He will, I predict, cross at the ford of Nogara; so set you forth, swinging wide of the armies, to approach this place from the north, travelling southward on the road from Culario. Then report to me again at the next favourable conjunction.'

The murmuring voice fell silent and the filmy vision faded, leaving Alcina alone and brooding.

Then came a thunderous knock, and in lurched Fadius. The Kothian had spent more of his time and Vibius Latro's money in a Messantian wineshop than was prudent. Arms out, he staggered towards Alcina, babbling:

'Come, my little passion flower! I weary of sleeping on the bare floor, and 'tis time you accorded your comrade the same kindness you extend to barbarian bullies—'

Alcina leaped to her feet and backed away. 'Have a care, Master Fadius!' she warned. 'I take not kindly to presumption from such a one as you!'

'Come on, my pretty,' mumbled Fadius. 'I'll not hurt you—'

Alcina's hand flicked to the bodice of her gown. As by magic, a slender dagger appeared in her jewelled hand. 'Stand back!' she cried. 'One prick of this, and you're a dying spy!'

The threat penetrated Fadius's sodden wits, and he recoiled from the blade. He knew the lightning speed with which the dancer-witch could move and stab. 'But – but – my dear little – '

'Get out!' said Alcina. 'And come not back until you're sober!'

Cursing under his breath, Fadius went. In the chamber, among the cages of roosting pigeons, Alcina rummaged in her chest for the garments in which she would set out upon the morrow.

VI

The Chamber
of Sphinxes

Between sunset and midnight, the men of Argos, rank upon rank, marched into camp amid ruffles of drums and rebel cheers. Salted Messantian meat, coarse barley bread and skins of ale from the rebels' dwindling stores were handed round to Baron Groder's starvelling regiment and Prospero's weary troop. Horses were watered, hobbled, and turned out to pasture on the lush grass, as the rebels and their new allies lit campfires and settled down to their evening repast. Soon the fitful glow of fires scattered about the Plain of Pallos rivalled the twinkling stars upon the plain of heaven; and the shouts and laughter of four thousand men, wafted northward on the evening breeze, crashed like the dissonant chords of a dirge on the ears of Procas's retreating regulars.

In the command tent, Prince Cassio, Captain Arcadio, and the rebel leaders gathered near Conan's bed to share a frugal meal and draft the morrow's plans.

'We'll all after them at dawn!' cried Trocero.

'Nay,' the young prince replied. 'The instructions from my royal father are explicit. Only if General Procas leads his forces further into our territory are we to join battle with him. The king hopes our presence will deter Procas from such rashness; and so it seems, since the Aquilonians are now in flight.'

Conan said nothing, but the volcanic blaze in his blue eyes betrayed his angry disappointment. The prince glanced at him, half in awe and half in sympathy.

'I comprehend your feelings, General Conan,' he said gently. 'But you must understand our position, too. We do

84

not wish to war with Aquilonia, which outnumbers us two to one. Indeed, we have risked enough already, giving haven to your force within our borders.'

With a hand that trembled from effort, Conan grasped his cup of ale and brought it slowly to his lips. Sweat beaded his forehead, as if the flagon weighed half a hundredweight. He spilled some of the contents, drank the rest, and let the empty vessel fall to the floor.

'Then let us pursue Procas on our own,' urged Trocero. 'We can harry him back across the Alimane; and every man we fell will be one fewer to oppose us when we raise Poitain. If the survivors stand to make a battle of it – well, victory lies ever on the laps of the fickle gods.'

Conan was tempted. Every belligerent instinct in his barbaric soul enticed him to send his men in headlong pursuit of the royalists, to worry them like a pack of hounds, to pick them off by ones and twos all the way back beyond the Alimane. The Rabirian range seemed designed by Destiny for just the sort of action he could wage against the outnumbering invaders. Cloven into a thousand gullies and ravines, those wrinkled hills and soaring peaks begged him to ambush every fleeing soldier.

But should Procas's troops turn to make a stand, Fate might not grant her guerdon to Conan's rebels. They were poor in provisions and weak in weaponry even now; and the regiment that Prospero had rescued were worn and weary, on gaunt, shambling mounts, after days of hiding out and foraging in the field. Moreover, a general who cannot ride a horse or wield a sword cannot greatly inspire his followers to deeds of dash and daring. Enfeebled as he still was by Alcina's poison, Conan knew full well that he had no choice except to remain in camp or to travel in a litter as a spectator at the fray.

As night slipped into misty dawn and trumpets sounded the reveille, Conan, supported by two squires, looked out across the waking camp and pondered his position. He must not let Procas get back to Aquilonia unscathed. At the same time, to overcome the mighty Border Legion, he must devise some unexpected manner of warfare – some innovation to give advantage to his lesser numbers. He required a force that was mobile and swiftly manœuvrable, yet able to strike the foe from a distance.

As Conan stared at the mustering men, his brooding gaze alighted upon a single Bossonian, who flung himself upon a horse and galloped towards the palisaded gate. He must bear a message to the sentries at the circumference of the camp, Conan mused, and that message must be urgent; for the fellow had not bothered to remove the unstrung bow that hung slantwise across his shoulders nor to discard the heavy quiver of arrows that slapped against his thigh.

Years of service with the King of Turan flooded Conan's memory. In that army, mounted archers formed the largest single contingent: men who could shoot their double-curved bows of horn and sinew from the back of a galloping steed as accurately as most men could shoot with feet firmly fixed upon the ground. Such a skill his Bossonian archers could not master without a decade of practice; and besides, the Bossonian longbow was much too cumbersome to be handled from horseback.

Suddenly, in his mind's eye, Conan saw a host of mounted archers pursuing the fleeing foe until, coming within range, they dismounted to loose shaft after deadly shaft, before spurring away when at last the goaded enemy turned to engage their tormentors. Conan's explosive roar of laughter startled his camp servants, who gaped like yokels at a circus while Captain Alaricus ran to waken the physician-priest.

When Dexitheus, clad in scanty clothing, rushed to Conan's tent, Conan grinned at his bewilderment.

'No,' he chuckled, 'the purple lotus has not addled my wits, my friend. But the lord Mitra, or Crom, or some such blessed god has given me an inspiration. Send someone post-haste to bid the Argossean leaders hither.'

When Prince Cassio and Captain Arcadio, already armed and armoured, plodded up the slope to the headquarters tent, Conan roared a greeting, adding: 'You say King Milo forbids you to attack the retreating Aquilonians. Does the royal fiat encompass your horses, too?'

'Our *horses*, General?' repeated Arcadio blankly.

Conan nodded impatiently. 'Aye, your beasts. Quickly, Captain, an answer, if you will. Our steeds – the few we have – are underfed, as you can see by counting their poor ribs. But yours are fresh and of an excellent breed. Lend us five hundred mounts, and we'll forswear the service of a single Argossean soldier to send Amulius Procas home with his tail between his legs.'

As Conan outlined his plan, Prince Cassio grinned. More and ever more he liked this grim-visaged barbarian from the North, who made war in ways as ingenious as implausible.

'Lend him five hundred horses, Arcadio,' he said. 'The king, my father, said naught of that.'

The Argossean officer clanked off to issue orders. And presently, below them on the flat where the Bossonian archers lined up for morning roll call, ten score Argossean wranglers led saddled horses into the field behind them. Trocero and Prospero converged upon the startled and disordered foot soldiers and by their authority restored them to disciplined ranks.

'Fetch me my stallion and strap me to the saddle,' growled Conan. 'I must explain my plan to those who'll carry it out.'

'General!' cried Dexitheus. 'You should not, in your present state –'

'Spare me your cautions, Reverence. For a month the men have seen me not and doubtless wonder if I'm still alive.'

As Conan's squires, with many helping hands, strained to boost Conan's massive body into the saddle, the Cimmerian chafed at the sluggishness that chained his mighty limbs. His blue eyes blazed with the fire of unconquerable will, and his broad brows drew together with the fury of his effort to drive vitality back into his flaccid thews. Strive as he would, the blood flowed but feebly through his numbed flesh; for Alcina had concocted the deadly draught with consummate care.

At length his squires strapped Conan to his saddle, he

raving oaths the while and calling upon his sombre Northern gods to avenge this foul indignity. And though the palsy shook his burly body, his eyes, seething with elemental fury, commanded every upturned face to show him neither courtesy nor pity, but only the respect that was his due.

All this Prince Cassio watched, held spellbound by amazement. Back in Messantia, the courtiers had sneered at Conan as a savage, an untutored barbarian whom the Aquilonian rebel nobles had unaccountably chosen to manage their revolt. Now the prince sensed the primal power of the man, his deep reservoirs of elemental vigour. He perceived the Cimmerian's driving purpose, his originality of thought, his dynamic presence – qualities that transformed nobles and common soldiers alike into willing captives of his personality. This man, thought Cassio, was created to command – was born to be a king.

Supported by a mounted squire on either side, Conan paced his charger slowly down the ranks towards the battalion of Bossonian archers. Although his face contorted with the effort, he managed to raise a hand in greeting as he passed row upon row of loyal followers. The men burst into frantic cheers.

Half a league to the north, a pair of royalist scouts, left behind to watch the rebel army, were breaking fast along the road that led to Saxula Pass. The cheers came faintly to their ears, and they exchanged glances of alarm.

'What betides yonder?' asked the younger man.

The other shaded his eyes. ' 'Tis too far to see, but something must have happened to hearten the rebel host. One of us had best report to General Procas. I'll go; you stay.'

The second speaker gulped his last bite, rose, untied his horse from a nearby tree, and mounted. The morning air echoed the fading drumbeat of hooves as he vanished up the road.

Quieting his men with a small motion of his upraised hand,

Conan addressed the lines of archers. They were selected, he told them, from the entire army to inflict destruction on the retreating invaders. They were to move on silent hooves against pockets of the enemy and then dismount and nock their shafts. Shooting from cover in twos and threes, they could pick off scores of fleeing men; and when at last the enemy turned at bay, they, unencumbered by heavy armour, could quickly remount and soon outdistance the heavy-laden Aquilonian knights sent in pursuit.

Each squad would be commanded by an experienced cavalryman, who would make certain that the beasts were well handled and would hold the horses while the archers were dismounted. As for those who had seldom ridden – here Conan smiled a trifle grimly – they had but to grip the saddle or the horse's mane; for such temporarily mounted infantry, fine horsemanship was unimportant.

Under the command of an Aquilonian soldier-of-fortune named Pallantides, who had once trained with Turanian horse-archers and who had lately deserted from the royalists, the newly mounted Bossonians swept out of the camp at a steady canter and headed north along the climbing road that led towards Aquilonia.

They caught up with the rear guard of the royalist army in the foothills of the Rabirians, short of Saxula Pass; for Procas's retreat was slowed by his baggage train and his companies of plodding infantry. Spying the enemy, the Bossonians spread out, eased their horses through the brush to shooting range, and then went to work. A score of royalist spearmen fell, screaming or silent, or cursed less lethal wounds, before the clatter of armoured horsemen told the rebel archers that Procas's cavalry was coming to disperse the attack and to cover his withdrawal. Thereupon the Bossonians unstrung their bows and, dashing back to their tethered beasts, silently mounted and scattered through the forest. Their only casualty was an injury to one archer who, unused to horseback, fell off and broke his collar-bone.

For the next three days, the Bossonians harried the retreating Aquilonians, like hounds snapping at the heels of fleeing criminals. They struck from the shadows; and when the royalists turned to challenge them, they were gone – hidden in a thousand hollows etched by wind and weather upon the wrinkled face of the terrain.

Amulius Procas and his officers cursed themselves hoarse, but little could they do. An arrow would whistle from behind a boulder. Sometimes it missed, merely causing the marching men to flinch and duck. Sometimes it buried itself in a horse's flank, inciting the stricken animal to rear and plunge, unseating its rider. Sometimes a soldier screamed in pain as a shaft transfixed his body; or a horseman, with a clang of armour, toppled from his saddle to lie where he fell. From the heights above, unseen in the gloaming, a sudden rain of arrows would slay or cripple thrice a dozen men.

Amulius Procas had few choices. He could not camp near Saxula Pass, because there little open ground and inadequate supplies of water could be found. Neither could he attack in close order, where his weight of numbers and armour would give him the advantage, because the enemy refused to close with him. If he threw his whole army against them, he could doubtless sweep away these pestilent rebels like chaff upon the wind; but such an action would carry him back to the Plain of Pallos and thus embroil him with the Argosseans.

So there was nothing for Amulius Procas to do but plod grimly on, sending out his light horse to drive away the enemy whenever they revealed their presence by a flight of arrows. Numerically his losses were trivial, only a fraction of the death toll of a joined battle. But the constant attrition depressed his men's morale; and the wind of chill foreboding, sweeping across his heart, whispered that King Numedides would not forget and still less forgive the failure of the expedition launched at the king's express command.

In the throat of Saxula Pass, an avalanche of boulders crashed down upon the hapless royalists. Procas glumly ordered the wreckage cleared, the smashed wagons abandoned, and the mortally wounded men and beasts mercifully put to the sword. On the far side of the pass, his troops moved faster, but the harassment continued unabated.

Procas realized that his Cimmerian opponent was a master of this irregular warfare; and he shook with shame that his enforced withdrawal had spurred the barbarian's fecund inventiveness. This stain upon his honour, he swore, he would wash out in rebel blood.

On the third day of the retreat, as the grey skies turned to lead, the disheartened, exhausted royalists gathered on the southern bank of the Alimane at the ford of Nogara. There for a time Procas lingered, tormented by indecision. Even though the floods of spring had subsided, the river's reach invited an attack when his fording men were least disposed to counter it. It would be a cruel jest of the capricious gods to ensnare the Aquilonian general in the very trap in which, not two months earlier, he had all but crushed the rebels. Moreover, to essay a crossing in the gloom of coming night would involve an almost certain loss of men and equipment.

Yet to pitch a camp on the Argossean side would doom sentries and sleeping men to death by flights of phantom arrows from the forest. Procas gnawed his lip. Since his troops could not effectively defend themselves against such tactics, the sooner he led them across the Alimane the safer they would sleep. Although the river was broad and swift, making the fords formidable, it would at least place his army beyond bowshots from the southern shore.

While these thoughts shambled through the mind of Amulius Procas, one of his officers approached the chariot in which he stood, atop a small rise along the river bank. The officer, a heavy-shouldered giant of a man – a Bossonian from his accent – with a surly expression on his coarse-featured face, saluted.

'Sir, we await your orders to begin the fording,' he said. 'The longer we stay, the more of our men will those damnable hidden archers wing.'

'I am aware of that, Gromel,' said the general stiffly. Then he heaved a sigh and made a curt gesture. 'Very well, get on with it! Naught's to be gained by loitering here. But it goes against my grain to let these starvelling rascals harry us home without repaying them in their own coin. Were it not for political considerations . . .'

Gromel raked the hills behind them with a contemptuous glance. 'Curse these politics, which tie the soldier's hands!' he growled. 'The cowards will not stand and fight, knowing we should wipe them out. So there is nothing for it save to gather on the soil of Poitain, there to stand ready to crush them if they essay the fords again.'

'We shall be ready,' said Procas sternly. 'Sound the trumpets.'

The retreat across ·the Alimane proceeded in good order, although night dimmed the twilight before the last company splashed into the river bed. As the men moved away from the southern bank, ten score archers, lurking in the undergrowth, stepped into view with bows strung and arrows nocked.

Procas had left his chariot to heave himself, grunting with pain from ancient wounds, into the saddle of his charger. Commanding a small rear guard of light horse, the dour old veteran was among the last to wade his steed into the darkling flood, while arrows from shore whistled past like angry insects.

In midstream the general suddenly exclaimed, clapping a hand to his leg. At his cry, the Bossonian officer who had addressed him earlier rode nigh and reined in. He opened thick lips to ask what was amiss, then spied the rebel arrow that had pierced the old man's thigh above the knee. A gleam of satisfaction flickered in Gromel's porcine eyes and quickly vanished; for he was a man implacably bent on pursuit of promotion, however he might attain it.

Stoically, Procas sat his steed across the river; but once amid the bushes that fringed the northern shore, he suffered his aides to lift him from the beast while Gromel trotted ahead to summon the surgeon.

After plucking forth the barb and binding the wound, the physician said: 'It will be many days, General, ere you will be well enough to travel again.'

'Very well,' said Procas stolidly. 'Pitch my tent on yonder hillock. Here we shall camp and let the rebels come to us, if they've got the stomach for it.'

Ghostly among the shadows of the trees nearby, a slender figure clad in the garments of a page, much worn and travel-stained, watched and listened. Had any viewer with catlike eyes perceived the swelling rondure of that youthful figure, he would have recognised a lithe and lovely woman. Now, with a mirthless smile, she unhitched her horse and quietly led the animal to a prudent distance from the camp that the Border Legion was hastily erecting.

That his rival, Amulius Procas, had been wounded during a cowardly retreat before a rabble would be pleasing news for Thulandra Thuu, thought the Lady Alcina. Now that the mighty Cimmerian was dead, Procas had served his purpose and could safely be sacrificed to her master's vaulting ambition. She must get word to the wizard as soon as the aspects of the stars and planets again permitted the use of her obsidian talisman. She melted into the darkness and vanished from the scene.

Bending towards his magical mirror of burnished obsidian, Thulandra Thuu learned with delight of the injury to General Procas. As the image of Alcina faded from the gleaming glass, the sorcerer thoughtfully stroked the bridge of his hawklike nose. Reaching out a slender hand, he raised a metal mallet and smote the skull-shaped gong that hung beside his iron throne, and its sonorous note echoed dully through the purple-shrouded chamber.

Presently the draperies drew aside, revealing Hsiao the Khitan. Arms tucked into the voluminous sleeves of his green silk robe, he bowed, silently awaiting his master's commands.

'Does the Count of Thune still wait upon me in the ante-chamber?' the sorcerer enquired.

'Master, Count Ascalante attends your pleasure,' murmured the yellow servant.

Thulandra Thuu nodded. 'Excellent! I will speak to him forthwith. Inform him that I shall receive him in the Chamber of the Sphinxes, and go yourself to notify the king that I shall presently request an audience upon urgent business of state. You have my leave to go.'

Hsiao bowed and withdrew, and the draperies fell back into place, concealing the door through which the Khitan had passed.

The Chamber of the Sphinxes, which Thulandra Thuu had converted to his own use from a disused room in the palace, was aptly named. Tomblike in its barrenness, it was walled and floored in roseate marble and contained no visible furnishings beyond a limestone seat, placed against the further wall. This seat, shaped like a throne, was upheld by a pair of stone supports carved in the likeness of feline monsters with human heads. This motif was repeated in the matching tapestries that hung in rich array against the wall behind the throne. Here, cunningly crafted in glittering threads, two catlike beasts with manlike faces, bearded and imperious, stared out with cold and supercilious eyes. The only light in this chill chamber was provided by a pair of copper torchères, the flames of which danced in the silver mirrors set into the wall behind them.

Not unlike the sphinxes was Ascalante, officer-adventurer and self-styled Count of Thune. A tall and supple man, elegantly clad in plum-coloured velvet, he prowled around the chamber with a feline grace. For all his military bearing and debonair deportment, his eyes, like those of the embroidered monsters, were cold and supercilious; but they were wary, too, and a trifle apprehensive.

For some time now, Ascalante had awaited an audience with the all-powerful sorcerer of unknown origin. Although Thulandra Thuu had recalled Ascalante from the eastern frontier and demanded his daily presence at court, the magician had let him cool his heels outside the audience chamber for several days. Now it might be that his fortunes were about to change.

Suddenly Ascalante froze, his hand instinctively darting to the hilt of his dagger. One of the tapestries lifted to reveal a narrow doorway, within which stood a slender, dark-skinned man, silently regarding him. The cool, amused intelligence behind those hooded eyes seemed capable of reading a man's thoughts as if they were painted on his forehead. Recovering his composure, Ascalante made a courtly obeisance as Thulandra Thuu entered the room. The sorcerer bore an ornately carven staff, which writhed with intertwined inscriptions in characters unknown to Ascalante.

Thulandra strode unhurriedly across the chamber and seated himself on the sphinx-supported throne. He acknowledged the other's bow with a nod and the shadow of a smile, saying: 'I trust you are well, Count, and that your enforced inactivity has not wearied you?'

Ascalante murmured a polite reply.

'Count Ascalante,' said the magician, 'your experience and accomplishments have not eluded those who serve as my eyes and ears in distant places. Neither, I may add, has your lust for high office, nor a certain lack of scruple as regards the means whereby you hope to attain it. I hasten to assure you that the king and I approve of your ambition and of your – ah – practicality.' .

'I thank you, my lord,' replied the count with a show of composure that aped the suavity of the sorcerer.

'I shall come directly to the point,' said Thulandra Thuu, 'for events move ever forward through the passing hours, and mortal men must scurry to keep abreast of them. Briefly, this is the situation: it has pleased His Majesty to withdraw his favour from the honourable Amulius Procas, commander of the Border Legion.'

Amazement burned in the inscrutable eyes of Ascalante, for the news astounded him. All knew that Procas was the ablest commander Aquilonia could put in the field, now that Conan had left the king's service. If anyone could subdue the restive barons in the North and crush the rebellion in the South, it was Amulius Procas. To remove him from command at such a time, before either menace had been obliterated, was madness.

'I can divine the feelings that your loyalty reins in,' purred Thulandra with a narrow smile. 'The fact is that our General Procas has led a rash and ill-planned raid across the Alimane, thus risking open war with Milo, King of Argos.'

'Forgive me, lord, but I find this almost impossible of credence,' said Ascalante. 'To invade a friendly neighbouring state without our monarch's express command is tantamount to treason!'

'It is precisely that,' smiled the sorcerer. 'And that the king imprudently did order a punitive expedition into Argos is a datum that, I fear, history will fail to record, since every copy of the document has strangely disappeared. You take my meaning, sir?'

Amusement gleamed in Ascalante's eyes. 'I believe I do, my lord. But pray continue.' The Count of Thune appreciated a subtle act of villainy much as a connoisseur of wines might savour a rare vintage.

'The general might have avoided censure,' Thulandra Thuu added with mock regret, 'if he had stamped out the last sparks of the rebellion; for the rumours you have heard about the self-styled Army of Liberation, now gathered north of the Rabirians, are true. An adventurer who called himself Conan the Cimmerian –'

'That giant of a man who last year led the Lion Regiment of Aquilonia to victory over the marauding Picts?' cried Ascalante.

'The same,' replied Thulandra. 'But time presses and affords us little leisure for profitless gossip, however diverting. Had General Procas shattered the rebel remnant and then retreated across the Alimane before King Milo learned of the incursion, all had been well. But Procas bungled the mission, stirred up the wrath of Argos, and fled from the field of battle without spilling a single drop of rebel blood. He so botched the fording of the Alimane that rebel archers targeted scores of our finest soldiers. And his errors were

compounded in Messantia by the blunders of a stupid spy
of Vibius Latro – a Zingaran named Quesado – whom His
Majesty had impulsively urged upon the diplomatic corps.

'The upshot was that, during the retreat, the general himself was wounded – so severely that, I fear, he is no longer
able to command. Fortunately for us, the rebel leader Conan
also perished. So to return to you, my dear Count – '

'To me?' murmured Ascalante, affecting an air of infinite
modesty.

'To yourself,' said the sorcerer with a sliver of a smile.
'Your service on the Ophirean and Nemedian frontiers, I
find, qualifies you to take command of the Border Legion,
which has fallen from the failing hands of General Procas
– or shortly will, once he receives this document.'

The sorcerer paused and withdrew from the deep sleeve
of his garment a scroll, richly embellished with azure and
topaz ribbons, upon which the royal seal blazed like a clot
of freshly shed blood.

'I begin to understand,' said Ascalante. And eagerness
welled up within his heart, like a bubbling spring beneath
a stone.

'You have long awaited the call of opportunity to ascend
to high office in the realm and earn the preferment of your
king. That opportunity approaches. But – ' and here Thulandra raised a warning finger and continued in a voice
sibilant with emphasis – 'you must fully understand me, Count
Ascalante.'

'My lord?'

'I am aware that the Herald's Court has not as yet
approved your assumption of the Countship of Thune, and
that certain – ah – irregularities surround the demise of your
elder brother, the late lamented count, who perished in a
"hunting accident".'

Flushing, Ascalante opened his lips to make an impassioned
protest; but the sorcerer silenced him with lifted hand and
a bland, uncaring smile.

'These are but minor disagreements, which shall be swept

away in the acclaim that greets the laurelled victor. I will see you well rewarded for your service to the crown,' Thulandra Thuu continued craftily. 'But you must obey my orders to the letter, or the County of Thune will never fall to you.

'I am aware that you have little actual experience in border warfare, or in commanding more men than constitute a regiment. The actual command of the Border Legion, then, I shall place in the hands of a certain senior officer, Gromel the Bossonian by name, who has been well blooded in our recent warfare against the Picts. I have long had Gromel under observation, and I plan to bind him to me with hopes of recompense. Therefore, while he shall deploy and order the actual battle lines, you will retain the nominal command. Is this quite understood?'

'It is, my lord,' hissed Ascalante between clenched teeth.

'Good. Now that Conan lies dead, you and Gromel between you can easily immobilise the remaining rebels south of the Alimane until the fractious horde disintegrates from hunger and lack of accomplishment.'

Thulandra Thuu proffered the scroll, saying: 'Here are your orders. An escort awaits you at the South Gate. Ride for the ford of Nogara on the Alimane with all dispatch.'

'And what, lord, if Amulius Procas refuses to accept my bona fides?' enquired Ascalante, who liked to make certain that he held all the winning pieces in any game of fortune.

'A tragic accident may befall our gallant general before your arrival to assume command,' smiled Thulandra Thuu. 'An accident which – when you officially report it – will be termed a suicide due to despondency over cowardice in the face of insubstantial foemen and repentance for provoking hostilities against a neighbouring realm. When this occurs, be sure to send the body home to Tarantia. Alive, Procas would not have been altogether welcome here; dead, he will play the leading role in a magnificent funeral.

'Now be on your way, good sir, and forget not to obey orders to be given to you from time to time by one Alcina, a trusted green-eyed woman in my service.'

Grasping the embossed scroll, Ascalante bowed deeply

and departed from the Chamber of Sphinxes.

Watching his departure, Thulandra Thuu smiled a slow and mirthless smile. The instruments that served his will were all weak and flawed, he knew; but a flawed instrument is all the more dispensable should it need to be discarded after use.

VII

Death in the Dark

For many days, the presence of the army of Amulius Procas on the far side of the Alimane deterred the rebels from attempts to ford the river. Although Procas himself, injured and unable to walk or ride, remained secluded in his tent, his seasoned officers kept a vigilant eye alert for any movement of the rebel forces. Conan's men marched daily up and down the river's southern shore, feinting at crossing one or another ford; but Procas's scouts remarked every move, and naught occurred to give pleasure to the Cimmerian or his cohorts.

'Stalemate!' groaned the restive Prospero. 'I feared that it might come to this!'

'What we require for our success,' suggested Dexitheus, 'is a diversion of some kind, but on a colossal scale – some sudden intervention of the gods, perchance.'

'In a lifetime devoted to the arts of war,' responded the Count of Poitain, 'I have learned to rely less upon the deities than on my own poor wits. Excuse me, Your Reverence, but methinks if any diversion were to deter Amulius Procas, it would be one of our own making. And I believe I know what that diversion well may be; for our spies report that the pot of my native county is coming to the boil.'

That night, with the approval of the general, a man clad all in black swam the deeper reaches of the Alimane, crept dripping into the underbrush, and vanished. The night was heavily overcast, dark and moonless; and a clammy drizzle herded the royalist sentries beneath the cover of the trees and shut out the small night sounds that might otherwise have alarmed them.

The swimmer in dark raiment was a Poitanian, a yeoman

of Count Trocero's desmesne. He bore against his breast an envelope of oiled silk, carefully folded, in which lay a letter penned in the count's own hand and addressed to the leaders of the simmering Poitanian revolt.

Amulius Procas did not sleep that night. The rain, sluiced against the fabric of his tent, depressed his fallen spirits and inflamed his aching wound. Growling barbarous oaths recalled from years spent as a junior officer along the frontiers of Aquilonia, the old general sipped hot spiced wine to ward off chills and fever and distracted his melancholy with a board game played against one of his aides, a sergeant. His wounded leg, swathed in bandages, rested uneasily on a rude footstool.

The grumble of thunder caused the army veteran to lift his grizzled head.

' 'Tis only thunder, sir,' said the sergeant. 'The night's a stormy one.'

'A perfect night for Conan's rebels to attempt a crossing of the fords,' said Procas. 'I trust the sentries have received instruction to walk their rounds, instead of lurking under trees?'

'They have been so instructed, sir,' the sergeant assured him. 'Your play, sir; observe that my queen has you in check.'

'So she has; so she has,' muttered Procas, frowning at the board. Uneasily he wondered why a cold chill pierced his heart at hearing those harmless words, 'my queen has you in check'. Then he scoffed at these womanish night fears and downed a swallow of wine. It was not for old soldiers like Amulius Procas to flinch from frivolous omens! But still, would that he had been in fettle personally to inspect the sentries, who inevitably grew slack in the absence of a vigilant commander . . .

The tent flap twitched aside, revealing a tall soldier.

'What is it, man?' asked Procas. 'Do the rebels stir?'

'Nay, General; but you have a visitor.'

'A visitor, you say?' repeated Procas in perplexity. 'Well, send him in; send him in!'

'It's "her", sir, not "him",' said the soldier. As Procas gestured for the entry of the unknown visitor, his partner at the board game rose, saluted, and left the tent.

Presently the soldier ushered in a girl attired in the vestments of a page. She had boldly approached the sentries, claiming to be an agent of King Numedides's ministers. None asked how she had travelled thither, being impressed by her icy air of calm authority and by the strange light that burned in her wide-set emerald eyes.

Procas studied her dubiously. The sigil that she showed meant little to him; such baubles can be forged or stolen. Neither gave he much credence to the documents she bore. But when she claimed to carry a message from Thulandra Thuu, his curiosity was aroused. He knew and feared the lean, dark sorcerer, whose hold over Numedides he had long envied, distrusted, and tried to counteract.

'Well,' growled Amulius Procas at length, 'say on.'

Alcina glanced at the two sentries standing at her elbows, with hands on sword hilts. 'It is for your ears only, my general,' she said gently.

Procas thought a moment, then nodded to the sentries. 'Very well, men; wait outside!'

'But, sir!' said the elder of the two, 'we ought not to leave you alone with this woman. Who knows what tricks that son of evil, Conan, may be up to—'

'Conan!' cried Alcina. 'But he's dead!' No sooner had she uttered those impetuous words than she would have gladly bitten off her tongue could she have thus recalled them.

The older sentry smiled. 'Nay, lass; the barbarian has more lives than a cat. They say he suffered a wasting illness in the rebel camp for a while; but when we crossed the river, there he was behind us on his horse, shouting to his archers to make hedgehogs of us.'

Amulius Procas rumbled: 'The young woman evidently thinks that Conan perished; and I am fain to learn the reason for her view. Leave us, men; I am not yet such a drooling dotard that I need fear a wisp of a girl.'

When the sentries had saluted and withdrawn, Amulius Procas said to Alcina with a chuckle: 'My lads seize every opportunity to stay in out of the rain. And now repeat to me the message from Thulandra Thuu. Then we shall investigate the other matters.'

Rain pounded on the tent, and thunder rolled as Alcina fumbled at the fastenings of the silken shirt she wore beneath her rain-soaked page's tunic. Presently she said:

'The message from my master, sir, is . . .'

A bolt of lightning and a crash of thunder drowned her following words. At the same time, she dropped her voice to just above a whisper. Procas leaned forward, thrusting his greying head to within a hand's breadth of her face in an effort to hear. She continued in that same sweet murmur:

'— that the time — has come —'

With the speed of a striking serpent, she drove her slender dagger into Amulius Procas's chest, aiming for the heart.

'— for you to die!' she finished, leaping back to escape the flailing sweep of the wounded general's arms.

True though her thrust had been, it encountered a check. Beneath his tunic, Procas wore a shirt of fine mesh-mail. Although the point of the dagger pierced one of the links and drove between the general's ribs, as the blade widened it became wedged within the link and so penetrated less than a finger's breadth. And, in her frantic struggle to wrench it free, Alcina snapped off the blade's tip, which remained lodged in the general's breast.

With a hoarse cry, the old soldier rose to his feet despite his injury and lunged, spreading his arms to seize the girl. Alcina backed away and, upsetting the taboret on which the candle stood, snuffed out the flame and plunged the tent into darkness deeper than the tomb.

Amulius Procas limped about in the ebon dark, until his strong hands chanced to grasp a handful of silken raiment. For a fleeting instant Alcina thought that she was doomed to die choking beneath the general's thick, gnarled fingers; but as the fabric ripped, the old soldier gasped and staggered. His injured leg gave way, and death rattled in his throat as he fell full-length across the carpet. The venom on Alcina's blade had done its work.

Alcina hastened to the entrance and looked out through a crack in the tent flap. A flash of lightning limned the two sentries, huddled in their sodden cloaks, standing like statues to the left and right. She perceived with satisfaction that the rumble of the storm had masked the sounds of struggle within the general's tent.

Fumbling in the darkness, Alcina discovered flint, steel and tinder, and, with great difficulty, relighted the candle. Quickly she examined the general's body, then curled his fingers around the jewelled hilt of her broken dagger. Darting back to the tent flap, she peered at the soldiers standing stiffly still and began to croon a tender song, slowly raising her voice until the flowing rhythm carried to the sentinels.

The song she sang was a kind of lullaby, whose pattern of sound had been carefully assembled to hypnotize the hearer. Little by little, unaware of the fragile, otherworldly music, the sentries slipped into a catatonic lethargy, in which they no longer heard the rain that spattered on their helmets.

An hour later, having eluded the guards at the boundaries of the camp, Alcina regained her own small tent on a wooded hilltop near the river. With a gasp of fatigue, she threw herself into the shelter and began to doff her rain-soaked garments. The shirt was torn – a ruin . . .

Then she clapped a hand to her breast, where had reposed the obsidian talisman; but there it lay no longer. Appalled, she realized that Procas, in seizing her in the darkness, had grasped the slender chain on which it hung and snapped it off. The glassy half-circle must now be lying on the rug that floored the general's tent; but how could she recover it? When they discovered their leader's body, the royalists would swarm out like angry hornets. And at the camp hard-eyed sentries would be everywhere, with orders instantly to destroy a black-haired, green-eyed woman in the clothing of a page.

Shivering with terror and uncertainty, Alcina endured the

angry rolls of thunder and the drumming fingers of the rain. But her thoughts raced on. Did Thulandra Thuu know that Conan had survived her poison? Her master had revealed no hint of such unwelcome knowledge that last time they conferred by means of the lost talisman. If the news of the Cimmerian's recovery had not yet reached the sorcerer, she must get word to him forthwith. But without her magical fragment of obsidian, she could report only by repairing to Tarantia.

Further black thoughts intruded on her mind. If Thulandra Thuu had known that Conan lived, would he have ordered her to slay Amulius Procas? Might he not be angry with her for killing the general, even though he had himself ordained the act, now that Procas's leadership was needed to save the royalist cause? Worse, might the sorcerer not punish her for failing to give the rebel chieftain a sufficient dose of poison? Worse of all, what vengeance might he not exact from her who lost his magical amulet? Stranded weaponless, without communication with her mentor, resourceless save for her puny knowledge of the elementary forms of witchcraft, Alcina lost heart and for a moment wavered between returning to Tarantia and fleeing to a foreign land.

But then, she reflected, Thulandra Thuu had always used her kindly and paid her well. She recalled his hinted promises of instruction in the higher arts of witchcraft, his talk of conferring on her immortality like his own, and – when he became sole ruler over Aquilonia, to reign forever – his assurance that she would be his surrogate.

Alcina decided to return to the capital and chance her master's wrath. Besides, being both beautiful and shrewd, she had a way with men, no matter what their station. Smiling, she slept, prepared to set forth with the coming of the light.

Towards dawn, an Aquilonian captain approached the general's tent to have him sign the orders of the day. The two sentries of the night before, wearily anticipating the conclusion of their tour of duty, saluted their superior before one stepped forward to open the tent flap and usher the captain in.

But General Procas would sign no further orders, save perchance in hell. He sprawled face-down in a pool of his congealing blood, clasping in his hand the stump of the slim-bladed poniard that had stilled the voice of Aquilonia's mightiest warrior.

The two soldiers turned over the corpse and stared at it. Procas's iron-grey hair, now dappled with dried blood, lay in disorder, partly masking his dormant features.

'I shall never believe our general took his own life,' whispered the captain, deeply moved. 'It was not his way.'

'Nor I, sir,' said the sentry. 'What man determined to kill himself would plunge a dagger into a shirt of mail? It must have been that woman.'

'Woman? What woman?' barked the captain.

'The green-eyed one I led here late last night. She said she brought a message from the king. See, there is one of her footprints.' The soldier pointed to an outline of a small, booted foot etched in dried mud upon the carpet. 'We urged the general to let us stay during the interview, but he ordered us out regardless.'

'What became of the woman?'

The sentry turned up helpless hands. 'Gone, I know not how. I assure you, sir, that she did not pass us on her way out. Sergius and I were wide awake and at our posts from the time we left the general till you came just now for orders. You can ask the watch.'

'Hm,' said the captain. 'Only a devil can vanish from the midst of an armed and guarded camp of war.'

'Then perhaps the devil is a woman, sir,' muttered the sentry, biting his lip. 'Look there on the rug: a half-moon of rock-glass, black as the depths of hell.'

The captain toed the bit of obsidian, then kicked it aside impatiently. 'Some fribbling amulet, such as the superstitious wear. Devil or no, we must not stand here babbling. You guard the general's body, whilst I call up a squad to search the camp and the surrounding hills. Sergius, fetch me a trumpeter! If I ever catch that she-devil . . .'

Alone in the tent, the sentry furtively searched among the shadows on the rug and found the amulet. He examined his find, tied the broken ends of chain together, and slipped it over his head. If the ornament was not much to look at, it might at least bring him good luck. Somebody must have thought so, and a soldier needs all the good fortune that the gods bestow.

Conan leaned above the rim of a great rock and studied the disposition of the royalist troops, still encamped along the northern bank of the Alimane. Only the day before, something unsettling had occurred among them; for there had been much shouting and noisy confusion. But from his eyrie not even the keen-eyed Cimmerian could discern the nature of the disturbance.

Keeping his eyes fixed on the scene across the river, Conan accepted a joint of cold meat from his squire and gnawed on it with a lusty appetite. He felt full of renewed vigour, now that he had shaken off the lingering effects of the poisoned wine; and the days of harrying the Border Legion home had much appeased his rage over the lost battle amid the waters of the Alimane, where so many of his faithful followers had perished in the swirling flood.

Years had passed since the Cimmerian adventurer had last fought a guerilla war – striking from the shadows, ambushing stragglers, hounding a stronger force from the security of darkness. Then he had commanded a brigand band in the Zuagir desert. Pleased he was that the skills were still with him, trammelled in his memory, razor-sharp in spite of long disuse.

Still, now that the enemy had crossed the Alimane and were encamped upon the further bank, the problems of the war he fought had changed again – and, thought the impatient Cimmerian, changed for the worse.

The hosts beneath the Lion banner could not ford the Alimane so long as the royalists stood ready to repel each assault. For such an attack to succeed in the face of vigorous resistance would require, as in scaling the walls of a fortress, overwhelming numbers; and these the rebels did not have. Nor could they rely upon guerilla tactics and the novel employment of mounted archers. Moreover, their supplies were running low.

Conan scowled as he moodily munched the cold meat. At least, he reflected, the troops of Amulius Procas displayed no inclination to recross the river to do battle. And for the twentieth time he pondered the nature of the event that, the day before, had so disturbed the orderly calm of the enemy camp.

The Border Legion had enlarged the open space on the further side of the river, where the Culario road met the water; they had felled trees, extending the clearing up and down the stream to make room for their camp. Beyond the camp, the forest was a wall of monotonous green, now that the springtime flowers on tree and shrub had faded. As Conan watched, a party of mounted men entered the encampment, and the song of trumpets foretold a visitation of some moment.

Conan shaded his eyes, frowned at the distant camp, and turned to his squire. 'Go fetch Melias the scout, and quickly.'

The squire trotted off, soon to return with a lean and leathery oldster. Conan glanced up, his face warm with greeting. Melias had served with Conan years before on the Pictish frontier. His eye was keener than any hawk's, and his moccasined feet slipped through dry underbrush as silently as a serpent.

'Who is it enters yonder camp, old man?' Conan enquired, nodding towards the royalist encampment.

The scout stared fixedly at the party moving down the company street. At length he said: 'A general officer – field rank, at any rate, from the size of his escort. And of the nobility, too, from his blazonry.'

Conan dispatched his page to fetch Dexitheus, who made a hobby of unravelling heraldic symbols. As the scout described the insignia embroidered on the newcomer's surcoat, the priest-physician rubbed his nose with a slow finger, as if to stimulate his memory.

'Methinks,' he said at last, 'that is the coat of arms of the Count of Thune.'

Conan shrugged irritably. 'The name is not unfamiliar to me, but I am sure I have never met the man. What know you of him?'

Dexitheus pondered. 'Thune is an eastern county of Aquilonia. But I have not encountered the present holder of the title. I recall some rumour – perhaps a year ago – of a scandal in connection with his accession; but further details I fail to recollect.'

Back at the rebel camp, Conan sought out the other leaders, to query them about the new arrival. But they could tell him little more than he already knew about the Count of Thune, save that the man had served as an officer on the peaceful eastern frontiers, with, so far as they knew, neither fabulous heroism nor crushing disgrace to his name.

By midafternoon, Melias reported that the troops of the Border Legion were ranked in parade formation and that, presently, the Count of Thune appeared and began to read aloud from documents bearing impressive seals and ribbons. Prospero and an aide slipped out of camp and, screened by foliage along the river bank, listened to the proceedings. Since a royalist sergeant repeated every phrase of the proclamation in a stentorian voice, which carried across the water, the astounded rebels learned that their adversary had died by his own hand and that Ascalante, Count of Thune, had been appointed in his place to command the Border Legion. This startling news they relayed with all dispatch to the other rebel chiefs.

'Procas a suicide?' growled Conan, bristling. 'Never, by Crom! The old man, for all he was my enemy, was a soldier through and through, and the best officer in all of Aquilonia. Such as Procas sell their lives dearly; they do not slough them off! I smell the stench of treachery in this; how say the rest of you?'

'As for myself,' muttered Dexitheus, fingering his prayer

beads, 'in this I see the sly hand of Thulandra Thuu, who long nursed hatred for the general.'

'Does none of you know more of this Count Ascalante?' demanded Conan. 'Can he lead troops in battle? Has combat seasoned him, or is he just another perfumed harger-on of mad Numedides?' When the others shook their heads, Conan added: 'Well, send your sergeants to enquire among the troops, whether any man of them has served beneath the count, and what manner of officer he was.'

'Think you,' asked Prospero, 'that this new commander of the Border Legion may unwittingly serve our cause?'

Conan shrugged. 'Perhaps; and perhaps not. We shall see. If Trocero's promised diversion comes to pass . . .'

Count Trocero smiled a secret smile.

The following morning, the rebel leaders, gathered on the lookout prominence, stared across the river in sombre fascination. While the Border Legion stood in parade formation, a small party of mounted men moved slowly through the camp and vanished up the Culario road. In their midst a pair of black horses, driven by General Procas's charioteer, trundled the general's chariot along at a slow and solemn pace. Across the rear of the vehicle was lashed a large wooden box or coffin.

Conan grunted: 'That's the last we shall ever see of old Amulius. If *he* had been king of Aquilonia, things would be quite different here today.'

A few nights later, when fog lay heavy on the surface of the Alimane, the black-clad swimmer, whom Count Trocero had sent across the river several days before, returned. Again he bore a letter sewn into an envelope of well-oiled silk.

That very night the Lion Banner rose against the silver splendour of the watchful moon.

VIII

Swords Across
the Alimane

For several months, the friends of Count Trocero had done their work, and well. In marketplace and roadside inn, in village and hamlet, in town and city, the whisper winged across the province of Poitain: 'The Liberator comes!'

Such was the title given to Conan by Count Trocero's partisans, men who remembered trembling tales of the giant Cimmerian from years gone by. They had heard how he thrust and cut amidst the silvery flood of Thunder River to break the will of the savage Picts, lest they swarm in their thousands across the border to loot and slay and ravish the Bossonian Marches. Poitanians who knew these stories now looked to the indomitable figure of Conan to wrest them from the clutches of their bloody tyrant.

For weeks, archers and yeomen and men-at-arms had filtered southward, ever southward, towards the Alimane. In the villages, men muttered over mugs of ale, their shaggy heads bent close together, of the invasion to come.

Now, at last, the Liberator neared. The moment loomed to free Poitain and, in good time, all of Aquilonia, prostrate now beneath the heavy heel of mad Numedides. The word so eagerly awaited had arrived in an oiled-silk envelope, stamped with the seal of their beloved count. And they were ready.

Chilled by the raw and foggy night, the sentinel, a youth from Gunderland, sneezed as he stamped his booted feet and slapped his shoulders. Sentry-go was a tedious tour of duty in the best of times, but on a damp night during a cold snap, it could be cursed uncomfortable.

If only he had not foolishly let himself be caught blowing kisses in the ear of the captain's mistress, thought the Gunderman gloomily, he might even now be carousing in the cheerful warmth of the sergeants' mess with his luckier comrades. What need, after all, to guard the main gate to the barracks of Culario on such a night as this? Did the commandant think an army was stealing upon the base from Koth, or Nemedia, or even far Vanaheim?

Wistfully he told himself, had he enjoyed the fortune of a landed sire and birth into the gentry, he would now be an officer, swanking in satin and gilded steel at the officers' ball. So deep was he in dreams that he failed to remark a slight scuff of feet behind him on the cobblestones. He was aware of nothing untoward until a leathern thong settled about his plump throat, drew quickly tight, and strangled him.

The officers' ball throbbed with merriment. Chandeliers blazed with the light of a thousand candles, which sparkled and shimmered in the silvered pier glasses. Splendid in parade uniforms, junior officers vied for the favours of the local belles, who fluttered prettily, giggling at the honeyed whispers of their partners, while their mothers watched benignly from rows of gilded chairs along the pilastered walls.

The party was past its peak. The royal governor, Sir Conradin, had made his requisite appearance to open the festivities and long since had departed in his carriage. Senior Captain Armandius, commandant of the Culario garrison, yawned and nodded over a goblet of Poitain's choicest vintage. From his red velvet seat, he stared down sourly upon the dancers, thinking that all this prancing, bowing and circling was a pastime fit for children only. In another hour, he decided, it would not seem remiss to take his leave. His thoughts turned to his dark-eyed Zingaran mistress, who doubtless waited impatiently for him. He smiled sleepily, picturing her soft lips and other charms. And then he dozed.

A servant first smelled smoke and thrust open the front

door, to see a pile of burning brush stacked high against the walls of the officers' barracks. He bawled an alarm.

In the space of a few breaths, the king's officers swarmed out of the burning building, like bees smoked out of their hive by honey-seeking boys. The men and their ladies, furious or bewildered, found the courtyard already full – crowded by silent, sombre men with grim eyes in their work-worn faces and naked steel in their sun-browned hands.

Alas for the officers; they wore only their daggers, more ornamental than useful, and so stood little chance against the well-armed rebels. Within the hour, Culario was free; and the banner of the Count of Poitain, with its crimson leopards, flew beside a strange new flag that bore the blazon of a golden lion on a sable field.

In a private room in Culario's best-regarded inn, the royal governor sat gaming with his crony, the Aquilonian tax assessor for the southern region. Both were deep in their cups, and consistent losses had rendered the governor surly and short tempered. Still, having escaped from the officers' ball, Sir Conradin preferred to shun his home for yet a while, knowing that his wife would accord him an unpleasant welcome. The presence of the sentry stationed in the doorway so fanned his irritation that he brusquely commanded the soldier to stand out of sight beyond the entrance to the inn.

'Give a man some privacy,' he grumbled.

'Especially when he's losing, eh?' teased the assessor. He guessed that the sentry would not have to brave the clammy mists for long, for Sir Conradin's purse was nearly empty.

Continuing their game, engrossed in the dance of ivory cubes and the whimsical twists of fortune, neither player noticed a dull thud and the sound of a falling body beyond the heavy wooden portal.

An instant later, booted feet kicked open the door of the inn; and a fierce-eyed mob of rustics, armed with clubs and rakes and scythes as well as more conventional weapons, burst in to drag the gamesters from their table to the crude gallows newly set in the centre of the market square.

The men of the Border Legion received their first warning that the province seethed with insurrection when an officer of the guard, yawning as he strolled about the perimeter of the camp to assure himself that every sentry stood alert and at his post, discovered one such sentinel slumbering in the shadow of a baggage wain.

With an oath, the captain sent his booted toe thudding against the shirker's ribs. When this failed to arouse the sleeper, the officer squatted to examine the man. A feeling of dampness on his fingers caused him to snatch away his hand; and he stared incredulously at the stain that darkened it and at the welling gash that bridged the fellow's throat. Then he straightened his back and filled his lungs to bellow an alarm, just in time to take an arrow through the heart.

Fog drifted across the rippling waters of the Alimane, to twist and coil around the boles of trees and the tents of sleeping men. Fog also swirled about the edges of the camp, where dark and sombre forests stood knee deep in purple gloom. The ghostly tendrils wreathed the trunks of immemorial oaks, and through the coils there drifted a wraithlike host of crouching figures in drab clothing, with knives in their hands and strung bows draped across their shoulders. These shadowy figures breasted the curtaining fog, going from tent to tent, entering softly, and emerging moments later with blood upon the blades of their silent knives.

As these intruders stole among the sleeping men, other dark figures struggled through the clutching waters of the Alimane. These, too, were armed.

Ascalante, Count of Thune, was roused from heavy slumber by a shapeless cry as of a man in agony. The cry was followed by a score of shouts, and then the horns of chaos blared across the camp. For a moment, the Aquilonian adventurer thought himself immersed in bloody dreams. Then there sounded through the dripping night the screams of men in mortal combat, the shrieks of the injured, the gurgle of the dying, the tramp of many feet, the hiss of arrows, and the clangour of steel.

Cursing, the count sprang half-naked from his cot, flung wide the tent flap, and stared out upon a scene of roaring carnage. Burning tents cast a lurid light across a phantasmagoria of indescribable confusion. Corpses lay tossed about and trampled in the slimy mud, like toys discarded by the careless hands of children. Half-clothed Aquilonian soldiers fought with the frenzy of despair against mail-suited men armed with spear, sword and axe, and others who plied longbows at such close range that every arrow thudded home. Royalist captains and sergeants strove heroically to force their pikemen into formation and to arm those who had issued unprepared from their shelters.

Then a terrible figure loomed up before the tent wherein the Count of Thune stood frozen with astonishment and horror. It was Gromel, the burly Bossonian, from whose thick lips poured a steady stream of curses. Ascalante blinked at him in amazement. The officer was clad in nothing but a loin cloth and a knee-length coat of mail. That mail was rent and hacked in at least a dozen places, baring Gromel's mightily muscled torso, which seemed to the fastidious count to be incarnadined with gore.

'Are we betrayed?' gasped Ascalante, clutching at Gromel's blood-encrusted sword arm.

Gromel shook off the grasping hand and spat blood. 'Betrayed or surprised, or both – by the slimy guts of Nergal!' growled the Bossonian. 'The province has risen. Our sentries are slain; our horses chased into the woods. The road north is blocked. The rebels have snaked across the river, unseen in these accursed fogs. Most of the sentries have had their throats cut by the countryfolk. We're caught between the two forces and helpless to fight back.'

'What's to be done, then?' whispered Ascalante.

'Flee for your life, man,' spat Gromel. 'Or surrender, as

I intend to do. Here, help me to bind up these wounds, ere
I bleed to death.'

First, hidden by the fog, Conan had led his pikemen across
the ford of Nogara. Once the fight had started, Trocero,
Prospero and Pallantides followed with the archers and
mounted troops. Before a wan moon broke through the
deep-piled clouds, the Count of Poitain found himself
engaged in a pitched battle; for enough of the Legionnaires
had gathered to make a wall of shields, behind which their
long spears bristled like a giant thorn bush. Trocero led his
armoured knights against this barrier of interlocking shields
and, after several unsuccessful tries, broke through. Then
the slaughter began.

The Numedidean camp was a makeshift affair, strung out
along the northern bank of the Alimane and backed against
the forest. Its elongated shape made it difficult to defend.
As a rule, Aquilonian soldiers built square encampments,
walled with earthworks or palisades of logs. Neither of these
defences was practicable in the present case, and thus the
camp of the Border Legion was vulnerable. The conformation
of the land, together with the complete surprise effected by
the Army of Liberation (as it came to be called) tipped the
balance in favour of the rebels, even though the Legionnaires
still outnumbered the combined forces of Conan and the
revolting Poitanians.

Besides, the morale of the Legion had declined, so that
Aquilonia's finest soldiers for once failed to deserve their
reputation. Ascalante had reported to his officers that their
former chief, Amulius Procas, died by his own hand, despon-
dent over his sorry showing in the Argossean incursion. The
soldiers of the Legion could scarcely credit this canard. They
knew and loved their old general, for all his strict discipline
and crusty ways.

To the officers and men, Ascalante seemed a fop and a
poseur. True, the Count of Thune had some experience with
the military, but in garrison duty only and on quiet frontiers.
And also true, any general stepping up to greatness over

battle-hardened senior officers needs time to cool the hot breath of rancour in those whom he commands. But the languid ways and courtly airs of the new arrival did little to conciliate his staff; and their discontent was wordlessly transmitted to the soldiers of the line.

The attack was well planned. When the Poitanian peasants had spilled the blood of the sentries, fired the tents, and driven off the horses from their makeshift corral, the sleeping troops, roused at last to their peril, formed ranks to challenge their attackers along the northern boundary of the camp. But when they were simultaneously battered from the south by Conan's unexpected forces, their lines of defence crumbled and the song of swords became a deathly clamour.

General Ascalante was nowhere to be found. Descrying a horse, the courtier had flung himself astride the unsaddled beast and, lacking spurs, had lashed the animal into motion with a length of branch torn from a nearby tree. He eluded the Poitanian foresters by a hair's breadth and galloped off into the night.

A cunning opportunist like Gromel might curry favour with the victors by surrendering himself and his contingent; but for Ascalante it was quite another matter. He had a noble's pride. Besides, the count divined what Thulandra Thuu would do when he learned of the débâcle. The sorcerer had expected his appointee to hold the rebels south of the Alimane – a task not too difficult under ordinary circumstances for a commander with a modicum of military training. But the magician's arts had somehow failed to warn him of the uprising of the Poitanians – an event that would have daunted an officer more seasoned than the Count of Thune. And now his camp was charred and cindered, and defeat was imminent. Ascalante, thus, could only quit the lieu and put as much distance as he could between himself and both the crafty rebel leader and the dark, lean necromancer in Tarantia.

Throughout the moonless night, the Count of Thune thundered through a tunnel of tall trees, and dawn found him nine leagues east of the site of the disaster. Spurred by the thought of Thulandra's incalculable wrath, he pushed ahead as fast as he dared go on his exhausted mount. There were places in the eastern deserts where, he hoped, even the vengeful sorcerer would never find him.

But as the hours passed, Ascalante conceived a fierce and abiding hatred of Conan the Cimmerian, on whom he laid the blame for his defeat and flight. In his heart the Count of Thune vowed some day in like manner to repay the Liberator.

Towards dawn Conan bestrode the Border Legion's ruined camp, receiving information from his captains. Hundreds of Legionnaires lay dead or dying, and hundreds more had sought the safety of the forest, whence Trocero's partisans were now dislodging them. But a full regiment of royalist soldiery, seven hundred strong, had come over to Conan's cause, having been persuaded by circumstances and a Bossonian officer named Gromel. The surrender of these troops – Poitanians and Bossonians, with a sprinkling of Gundermen and a few score other Aquilonians among them – pleased the Cimmerian mightily; for seasoned, well-trained professionals would bolster his fighting strength and stiffen the resolve of his motley followers.

A shrewd judge of men, Conan suspected Gromel, whom he had briefly known along the Pictish frontier, of being both a formidable fighter and a wily opportunist; but opportunism is forgivable when it serves one's turn. And so he congratulated the burly captain on his change of heart and appointed him an officer in the Army of Liberation.

Squads of weary men laboured to strip the dead of usable equipment and stack the corpses in a funeral pyre, when Prospero strode up. His armour, splashed with dried blood, was ruddy in the roseate light of dawn, and he seemed in rare good humour.

'What word?' asked Conan gruffly.

'Nothing but good, General,' grinned the other. 'We have captured their entire baggage train, with supplies and weapons enough for twice our strength.'

'Good work!' grunted Conan. 'What of the enemy's horses?'

'The foresters have rounded up the beasts they let run free, so we have mounts again. And we have taken several thousand prisoners, who threw down their arms when they saw their cause was hopeless. Pallantides fain would know what he's to do with them.'

'Offer them enlistment in our forces. If they refuse, let them go where they will. Unarmed men can harm us not,' said Conan indifferently. 'If we do win this war, we shall need all the good will we can muster. Tell Pallantides to let each choose his course.'

'Very well, General; what other orders?' asked Prospero.

'We ride this morn for Culario. Trocero's partisans report there's not a royalist still under arms between here and the town, which waits to welcome us.'

'Then we shall have an easy march to Tarantia,' grinned Prospero.

'Perhaps, and perhaps not,' Conan replied, narrowing his lids. 'It will be days before news of the royalist rout arrives in Bossonia and Gunderland and the garrisons there head south to intercept us. But they will come in time.'

'Aye. Under Count Ulric of Raman, I'll wager,' said Prospero. Then, as Trocero joined his fellow officers, he added: 'What is your guess, my lord Count?'

'Ulric, I have no doubt,' said Trocero. 'A pity we missed our meeting with the northern barons. They would have held him back for quite a while.'

Conan shrugged his massive shoulders. 'Prepare the men to move by noon. I'll take a look at Pallantides's prisoners.'

A short while later, Conan stalked down the line of disarmed royalist soldiery, stopping now and then to ask a sharp question: 'You wish to serve in the Army of Liberation? Why?'

In the course of this inspection, his eye caught the reflected sparkle of the morning sun on the hairy chest of a ragged prisoner. Looking more closely, he perceived that the light bounced off a small half-circle of obsidian, hung on a slender chain around the man's burly neck. For an instant Conan stared, struggling to remember where it was that he had seen the trinket. Taking the object between thumb and forefinger, he asked the soldier with a hidden snarl:

'Where did you get this bauble?'

'May it please you, General, I picked it up in General Procas's tent the morning after the general was – after he died. I thought it might be an amulet to bring me luck.'

Conan studied the man through narrowed lids. 'It surely brought no luck to General Procas. Give it to me.'

The soldier hastily stripped off the ornament and, trembling, handed it to Conan. At that moment Trocero approached, and Conan, holding up the object to his gaze, muttered. 'I know where I have seen this thing before. The dancer Alcina wore it around her neck.'

Trocero's eyebrows rose. 'Aha! then that explains –'

'Later,' said Conan. And nodding to the prisoner, he continued his inspection.

As the level shafts of the morning sun inflamed the clouds that lingered in the eastern sky, Conan's baggage train and rear guard lumbered across the Alimane; and soon thereafter the Army of Liberation began its march across Poitain to Culario and thence towards great Tarantia and the palace of its kings. To tread the soil of Aquilonia after so many months of scaling crags in a lost and hostile land heartened the rebel warriors. Bone-weary as they were after a night of slaughter, they bellowed a marching song as they threaded their way north among the towering Poitanian oaks.

Ahead, swifter than the wind, flew the glad tidings: The Liberator comes! From farm and hamlet to town and city, it winged its way – a mere whisper at first, but swelling as it went into a mighty shout – a cry that monarchs dread, presaging as it does the toppling of a throne or the downfall of a dynasty.

Conan and his officers, pacing the van on fine horseflesh, were jubilant. The progress through Count Trocero's demesne would be, as it were, on eagles' wings. The nearest royalist forces, unapprised of their arrival, lay several hundred leagues away. And since Amulius Procas was in his grave, they had no enemy to fear until they reached the very gates of fair Tarantia. There they would find the city portals locked and barred against them, this they knew; and the Black Dragons, the monarch's household guard, in harness to defend their king and capital. But because the people stood behind them and a throne lay before, they would hack down all defences and trample every foe.

In this the rebels were mistaken. One foe remained of whom they knew but little. This was the sorcerer Thulandra Thuu.

In his purple-pendant oratory, lighted by corpse-tallow candles, Thulandra Thuu brooded on his sable throne. He stared into his obsidian mirror, seeking by sheer intensity of purpose to wrest from the opaque pane bright visions of persons and events in distant places. At length with a small sigh, he settled back and rested his tired eyes. Then, frowning, he once again studied the sheet of parchment on which, in his spidery hand, were inscribed the astrological aspects he deemed conducive to communication by this occult means. He peered at the gilded crystal water clock and found no error of day or hour to explain his unsuccess. Whatever the cause, Alcina had failed to commune with him at the appointed time, now and for many days gone by.

A knock disturbed his melancholy meditation. 'Enter!' said Thulandra Thuu through lips livid with frustration.

The drapery parted, and Hsiao stood on the marble threshold. Bowing, the Khitan intoned in his quavering voice: 'Master, the Lady Alcina would confer with you.'

'Alcina!' The sharpness of the sorcerer's tone betrayed his agitation. 'Show her in at once!'

The hangings fell together silently, then parted once again. Alcina staggered in. Her page's garb, tattered and torn, was grey with dust and caked with sun-dried mud. Her black hair formed a tangled web around a face stiff with soil and apprehension. She dragged weary feet, scarce able to support her drooping frame. The beautiful girl, who had gallantly set off for Messantia, now seemed a worn woman in the winter of her years.

'Alcina!' cried the wizard. 'Whence come you? What brings you here?'

In a scarcely audible whisper, she replied: 'Master, may I sit? I am fordone.'

'Be seated, then.' As Alcina sank down upon a marble bench and closed her eyes, Thulandra Thuu projected his sibilant voice across the echoing chamber: 'Hsiao! Wine for Mistress Alcina. Now, good wench, relate all that has befallen you.'

The girl drew a sobbing breath. 'I have been eight days on the road, scarce halting to snatch a cat nap and a bite to eat.'

'Ah, so! And wherefore?'

'I came to say – to tell you – that Amulius Procas is dead –'

'Good!' said Thulandra Thuu, pinwheels of light dancing in his hooded eyes.

'– but Conan lives!'

At this astounding information, the sorcerer for the second time that day lost his composure. 'Set and Kali!' he cried. 'How did that happen? Out with it, girl; out with it!'

Before answering, Alcina paused to sip from the cup of saffron wine that Hsiao handed her. Then, haltingly, she recounted her adventures in the camp of the Border Legion – how she stabbed Procas; how she learned that Conan lived; and how she escaped the guard.

'And so,' she concluded, 'fearing that you knew not of the barbarian's miraculous survival, I deemed it my duty to report to you forthwith.'

Brows drawn in a ferocious frown, the sorcerer contemplated Alcina with his hypnotic gaze. Then he purred with the controlled rage of an angry feline: 'Instead of undertaking this weary journey, why did you not withdraw a prudent distance from the Legion's camp, and commune with me at the appropriate hour by means of your fragment of yonder mirror?'

'I could not, Master.' Alcina wrung her hands distractedly.

'Wherefore not?' Thulandra Thuu's voice suddenly jabbed like a thrown knife. 'Have you mislaid the table of positions of the planets, with which I did supply you?'

'Nay, my lord; it's worse than that. I lost my fragment of the mirror – I lost my talisman!'

Lips drawn back in a snarl, Thulandra uttered an ophidian hiss. 'By Nergal's demons!' he grated. 'You little fool! What devil of carelessness possessed you? Are you mad? Or did you set your silly heart on some lusty lout, like unto a she-cat in heat? For this I will punish you in ways unknown to mortal men! I will not only flog your body but flay your very soul! You shall live the pains of all your previous lives, from the first bit of protoplasmal slime up through the worm, the fish, and the ape! You shall beg me for death, but –'

'Pray, Master, do but listen!' cried Alcina, falling to her knees. 'You know men's lusts mean naught to me, save as I rouse them in your service.' Weeping, she told of the death struggle in the dark with Amulius Procas and of her later discovery of the loss of the talisman.

Thulandra Thuu bit his lip to master his rising wrath. 'I see,' he said at length. 'But when striking for great prizes, one cannot afford mistakes. Had your dagger travelled true, Procas would not have lingered long enough to seize your amulet.'

'I knew not that he wore a shirt of mail beneath his tunic. Can you not cut another fragment from the master mirror?'

'I could, but the enchantment of the fragment for transmitting distant messages is such a tedious process that the war were over ere it was completed.' Thulandra Thuu stroked his sharp chin. 'Did you make certain of Procas's death?'

'Yes. I felt his pulse and listened for his heart beat.'

'Aye. But you did not so with the Cimmerian! That was the greater error.'

Alcina made a gesture of despair. 'I served him with sufficient poison to have slain two ordinary men; but betwixt

his great size and the unnatural vitality that propelled him
. . .' She drooped abjectly at her master's feet and let her
voice trail off.

Thulandra Thuu rose; and towering above the trembling
girl, pointed a skinny forefinger towards heaven. 'Father Set,
can none of my servants carry out my simplest demand?'
Then, turning his sudden anger on the huddled girl, he
added: 'Little idiot, would you feed a boarhound on a lap-
dog's rations?'

'Master, you warned me not, and who am I to calculate
the grains of lotus venom needed for a giant?' Alcina's voice
rose and fury rode upon it. 'You sit in comfort in your palace,
whilst this poor servant courses the countryside in good and
evil weather, risking her skin to do your desperate deeds.
And not a kindly word have you to offer her!'

Thulandra Thuu spread his arms wide, palms upturned
in a gesture of forgiveness. 'Now, now, my dear Alcina, let
us speak no ill of one another. When allies part, the enemy
wins the battle by default. If I ask you to poison another of
my foes, I'll send along a clerk skilled in reckoning to
calculate the dose.'

He seated himself with a thin and rueful smile. 'Truly,
the gods must laugh like fiends at the irony of it. Having
sent Amulius Procas to whatever nether world the Fates
decreed, I earnestly wish that the old ruffian were alive again;
for on none but him can I rely to defeat the barbarian and
his rebel following.

'I thought that Ascalante and Gromel could together
thwart the insurgents' efforts to cross the Alimane; and so
they could have, were not Conan in command. Now I must
find an abler general for the Border Legion. This needs some
thinking on. Count Ulric of Raman has the Army of the
North in Gunderland, watching the Cimmerians. An able
commander, he; but the moon must wax and wane ere he
receives an order and rides the length of Aquilonia. Prince
Numitor lies closer on the Pictish frontier, but—'

Hsiao's tactful knock echoed like a tiny brazen bell.
Entering, he said: 'A pigeon-borne dispatch from Messantia,

Master, newly received by Vibius Latro.' Bowing, he handed the small scroll to the wizard.

Thulandra Thuu rose and held the scroll close to one of the huge candles, and reading, pressed his lips together until his mouth became a thin slit in his dusky face. At last he said:

'Well, Mistress Alcina, it seems the gods of my far distant island are careless of the welfare of their favoured child.'

'What has befallen now?' asked Alcina, rising to her feet.

'Prince Cassio, quoth Fadius, has sent a messenger from the Rabirian Mountains back to his sire in Messantia. Conan, it seems, fully recovered from an illness that struck him down, has crossed the Alimane and, with the aid of Poitanian lords and peasants, has utterly destroyed the Border Legion. Senior Captain Gromel and his men have deserted to the rebels; Ascalante may have fled, for neither he nor his exanimate body can be found.'

The wizard crumpled the missive and glared at Alcina; and the eyes he fixed upon her burned red with a rage such as she had never seen in any living eyes. He snarled: 'Betimes you tempt me, wench, to snuff out your miserable life, as a man extinguishes a lighted candle. I have a silent spell that turns mine enemy into a petty pile of ashes, with never a flame nor a plume of smoke –'

Alcina shrank away and crossed her arms upon her breast, but there was no escape from the sorcerer's hypnotic stare. Her body burned as from the licking tongues of flame that lapped the open door of a furnace. The magical emanations pierced her inmost being, and she closed her eyes as if to shut out the cruel radiations. When she opened them once more, she threw up her hands to ward off a blow and shrieked hysterically.

Where the sorcerer had stood, now reared a monstrous serpent. From its upraised head, swaying on a level with her own, slit-pupilled eyes poured maleficent rays into her soul, while a reptilian stench inflamed her nostrils. The scaly jaws gaped wide, revealing a pair of dagger-pointed fangs as the great head lunged towards her. Flinching, she blinked again;

and when she ventured to open her eyes, it was Thulandra Thuu who stood before her.

With a crooked smile on his narrow face, the wizard said: 'Fear not, girl; I do not wantonly blunt my tools whilst they still possess a cutting edge.'

Still shuddering, Alcina recovered herself enough to ask: 'Did – did you in truth take the form of a serpent, Master, or did you but cast an image of reality upon me?'

Thulandra Thuu evaded her question. 'I did but remind you which of us is master here and which apprentice.'

Alcina was content to change the subject. Pointing to the crumpled parchment, she asked: 'How came Fadius by Prince Cassio's information?'

'Milo of Argos declared a public celebration, and the reason was no secret. It is plain which side the old fool favours. And one item more: Milo ordered that clodpate Quesado banished from his kingdom, and our would-be diplomat was last seen travelling with an escort of Milo's household guard along the road to Aquilonia. I shall urge Vibius Latro to set the fellow working as a collector of offal; he is good for nothing else.

'And now, perhaps, our meddlesome mad king will leave affairs of state to me and confine himself to his besotted pleasures. I must ponder my next move in this board game with Fate, wherein a kingdom is the prize. And so, Alcina, you have my leave to go. Hsiao will provide you with food, drink, a much-needed bath, and woman's raiment.'

The league-long glittering river that was the Army of Liberation wound around tree-crowned hills, past fields and steads, and up to the gates of Culario. Conan, in the lead, reined in his black stallion at the sight of the gaping opening. From the gate towers flapped flags bearing the crimson leopards of Poitain; but the black heraldic eagle of Aquilonia was nowhere to be seen. Inside the city walls people lined both sides of the narrow street. In Conan's agile mind stirred the barbarian's suspicion of the trickery of civilised men.

Turning to Trocero, who rode a white gelding at his

side, Conan muttered: 'You're certain it's not a royalist trap they've set for us?'

'My head on it!' replied the count fervently. 'I know my people well.'

Conan studied the scene before him and rasped: 'Me thinks I'd best not look too much the conqueror. Wait a little.'

He unbuckled the chin strap of his helmet, pulled off the headpiece, and hung it on the pommel of his saddle. Then he dismounted with a clank of armour and strode towards the gate on foot, leading his horse.

Thus Conan the Liberator entered unpretentiously into Culario, nodding gravely to the citizens ranked on either side. Petals of fragrant flowers showered upon him; cheers resounded down the winding corridor. Following him on horseback, Prospero pulled to Trocero and whispered in his comrade's ear: 'Were we not fools the other night to wonder who should succeed Numedides?'

Count Trocero replied with a wry smile and a shrug of his iron-clad shoulders as he raised a hand in salutation to his fond and loyal subjects.

In his sanctum, Thulandra Thuu bent over a map, unrolled upon a taboret with weights of precious metals holding its edges down. He addressed himself to Alcina, now well rested from her journey and resplendent in a flowing robe of yellow satin, which clung to her fine-moulded body and glorified her raven hair.

'One of Latro's spies reports that Conan and his army are in Culario, resting from their battle and forced march. In time they will strike north, following the Khorotas to Tarantia.' He pointed with a long, well-pared fingernail. 'The place to stop them is at the Imirian Escarpment in Poitain, which lies athwart their path. The only force that has both weight and time enough to accomplish such a task is Prince Numitor's Royal Frontiersmen, based at Fort Thandara in the Westermarck of Bossonia.'

Alcina peered at the map and said: 'Then should you not order Prince Numitor to march south-east with all dispatch, taking all but a small garrison?'

The wizard chuckled drily. 'We shall make a general of you yet, good wench. The rider bearing that message in his pouch set off ere dawn.' Thulandra Thuu then measured off distances with his fingers, rotating his hand as if it were a draughtsman's compass. 'But, as you see, if Conan marches within the next two days, Numitor can in no way reach the escarpment in advance of him. We must cause him to delay.'

'Yes, Master, but how?'

'I am not unacquainted with weather magic and can control the spirits of the air. I shall contrive a scheme to hold the Cimmerian in Culario. Fetch hither yonder powders and potions, girl, and we shall test the power of my wizardry.'

Conan stood on the city wall beside the newly elected mayor of Culario. The day had been fair when they began their promenade; but now they gazed at an indigo sky across which clouds of leaden grey rolled in endless procession.

'I like it not, sir,' said the mayor. 'The summer has been wet, and this looks like the start of another spell. Too much rain can be as bad for the crops as none at all. And here it comes!' he finished, wiping a large drop from his forehead.

As the two men descended the spiral stair that wound around the tower, an agitated Prospero confronted them. 'General!' he cried. 'You slipped away from your bodyguard again!'

'By Crom, I like to get off by myself sometimes!' growled Conan. 'I need no nursemaid looking after me.'

'It is the price of power, General,' said Prospero. 'More than our leader, you've become our symbol and our inspiration. We must guard you as we would our banner or another sacred relic; for if the enemy could strike you down, his fight were three-fourths won. I assure you, spies of Vibius Latro lurk in Culario, watching for a chance to slip a poison into your wine, or a poniard between your ribs.'

'Those vermin!' snorted Conan.

'Aye, but you can die from such a creature's sting as readily as any common man. Thus, General, we have no choice but to cosset you as carefully as a newborn prince. These trifling inconveniences you must learn to endure.'

Conan heaved a gusty sigh. 'There's much to be said for the life of a footloose wanderer, such as once I was. Let's back to the governor's palace ere this cloudburst wash us all away.'

Conan and Prospero strode swiftly over the cobblestones, the stout mayor panting to keep pace. Overhead, a meandering crack of violet light cleft the sky, and thunder crashed like the roll of a thousand drums. The rain came down in sheets.

IX

The Iron Stallion

While Poitain writhed beneath the lash of the most violent storm in the memory of living men, a benign sun smiled on fair Tarantia. Standing in its salubrious rays on a palace balcony, Thulandra Thuu, attended by Alcina and Hsiao, looked out across the gently rolling fields of central Aquilonia, where summer wheat was ripening into spears of gold. To the dancer, now young and beautiful once more, with jewels atwinkle in her night-black hair and a gown of clinging satin sheathing her shapely form, the wizard said:

'The wheel of heaven reveals to me that the spirits of the air have served me well. My storm progresses apace; and after it subsides, the southern roads and every ford will be impassable. Numitor hastens from the Westermarck, and I must forth to join him.'

Alcina stared. 'You mean to travel to the field of battle, Master? Ishtar! That's not your wont. May I ask why?'

'Numitor will be outnumbered by the rebel forces; and despite forced marches, Ulric of Raman cannot reach Poitain until at least a fortnight after the prince arrives. Moreover, Prince Numitor is but an honest blockhead – doubtless the reason why our knavish king has let his cousin live when he has slain or exiled all his other kin. Nay, I cannot trust the prince to hold the Imirian Escarpment until Count Ulric arrives. He will require the assistance of my arcane arts.'

The sorcerer turned to his servant, the inscrutable slit-eyed one who had followed him from lands beyond the seas. 'Hsiao, prepare my chariot and gather the necessaries for our journey. We shall depart upon the morrow.'

Bowing, the man withdrew. Turning to Alcina, Thulandra Thuu continued: 'Since the spirits of the air have well obeyed me, I shall discover what the spirits of the earth will do to aid my cause. And you, good wench, I leave here as my deputy.'

'Me? No, Master; I lack the skills to take your place.'

'I will instruct you. First, you will learn to use the Mirror of Ptahmesu to commune with me.'

'But we are without the necessary talisman!'

'I can project images by the propellant power of my mind, though you could not. Come, we have no time to waste.'

From the royal paddocks Hsiao led out the single horse that drew his master's carriage. To a casual observer, the animal appeared to be a large black stallion; but a closer inspection of its hide revealed a strange, metallic sheen. The beast, moreover, neither pawed the ground nor lashed its tail at flies. In fact, no flies alighted on it, although the stable yard buzzed with their myriad wings. The stallion stood quiescent until Hsiao uttered a command unintelligible to any who might hear it; then the creature obeyed him instantly.

Hsiao now led the ebon stallion to the carriage house and backed it into the stall where stood Thulandra's chariot. When a careless hoof struck against one of the lowered carriage shafts, a metallic ring reverberated through the silent air.

The vehicle, a boxlike two-wheeled cart, lacquered in vermillion and emblazed with a frieze of writhing serpents worked in gold, was furnished with a seat across the back. A pair of carven posts, upthrust on either side, supported an arched wooden frame, covered with canvas. No ordinary cover this; it was embroidered with strange symbols beyond the ken of all who gazed upon it, save that the astute among them might discern the likeness of the moon and the major constellations of the southern hemisphere.

Into the chest beneath the seat of this singular vehicle, Hsiao placed all manner of supplies, and on the broad expanse above, he piled silken cushions in profusion. And as he worked, he hummed a plaintive song of Khitai, full of curious quarter-tones.

Conan and Trocero watched the sheeting rain from the governor's mansion. At length Conan growled: 'I knew not that your country lay at the bottom of an inland sea, my lord.'

The count shook his head. 'Never in half a century of living have I seen a storm of such intensity. Naught but sorcery could account for it. Think you Thulandra Thuu—'

Conan clapped his companion on the shoulder. 'You Aquilonians see magic lurking in every passing shadow! If you stub your toe, it's Thulandra's doing. In my dealings with these wizards, I've seldom found them so formidable as they would wish us to believe . . . Aye, Prospero?' he added, as the officer bustled in.

'The scouts have returned, General, and report all roads are utterly impassable. Even the smallest creeks are bursting into raging torrents. It were useless to send the column forward; they'd not advance a league beyond the city.'

Conan cursed. 'Your suspicion of that he-witch in Tarantia begins to carry weight, Trocero.'

'And we have visitors,' continued Prospero. 'The northern barons, who set out for home before we reached Culario, have been overtaken by the storm and forced to return hither.'

A smile illumined Conan's dark, scarred face. 'Thank Crom, good news at last! Show them in.'

Prospero ushered in five men in damp woollen travelling garments of good quality, mud-splattered from top to booted toe. Trocero presented the Baron Roaldo of Imirus, whose demesne lay in northern Poitain. A former officer in the royal army, this hardy, grey-haired noble had guided the other barons and their escorts to Culario and now introduced them to the Cimmerian.

Conan judged the lordlings to be men of divers characters: one stout, red-faced and full of boisterous good humour; another slim and elegant; still another fat and obviously privy to the pleasures of the table and the jug; and two of sombre mien and given to few words. Differing though they did among themselves, all heartily supported the rebellion; for their tempers were rubbed raw by Numedides's grasping tax collectors, and their ancient pride affronted by the royal troops stationed on their demesnes to wrest a yearly tribute from landowner and peasant. They avidly desired the downfall of the tyrant, and their questing gaze sought to discover Numedides's successor, so they might court their future monarch's favour.

After the barons had rested and donned fresh raiment, Conan and his friends heard their tally of complaints and drew out their hidden hopes. Conan promised little, but his sympathetic demeanour left each with the impression that, in a new regime, he would occupy a position of importance.

'Be warned, my lords,' said Conan, 'Ulric, Count of Raman, will move his troops across your lands as he travels south to confront our rebel army.'

'What troops does that greybeard count command?' snorted Baron Roaldo. 'A ragtail lot, I'll warrant. The Cimmerian frontier has long been peaceful and needs but a weak force to keep it safe.'

'Not so,' replied the Count of Poitain. 'I am informed that the Army of the North is nearly up to strength and boasts veterans of many a border clash. Indeed, Raman himself is a master strategist who escaped from the sack of Venarium, many years ago.'

Conan smiled grimly. As a stripling, he had joined the wild Cimmerian horde that plundered Fort Venarium, but of this he made no mention. Instead, he told the northern barons:

'Numedides will, I doubt not, send troops from the Westermarck; and being nearer, they will arrive the sooner. You must harry these northern contingents in a delaying action, at least until we rout the Bossonian royalists.'

Count Trocero eyed the barons keenly. 'Canst raise a fighting force without alerting the king's men stationed amongst you?'

Said Baron Ammian of Ronda: 'Those human grass-hoppers swarm only at harvest time to consume the fruit of our labours. They'll not arrive, the gods willing, for another month or two.'

'But,' argued the fat Baron Justin of Armavir, 'such a conflict, waged on our lands, will ruin both our purses and our people. Perchance we can delay Sir Ulric, but only till he burns our fields, scatters our folk and wrecks vengeance on our persons.'

'If General Conan fails to take Tarantia, we are beggared in any case,' countered the hard-featured Roaldo. 'Word will soon reach the tyrant's spies that we have joined the rebel cause. Better to game for a golden eagle than for a copper penny.'

'He speaks sooth,' said Ammian of Ronda. 'Unless we topple the tyrant, we shall all have our necks either lengthened or shortened, no matter what we do. So let us dare the hazard, and from encompassing dangers boldly pluck our safety!'

At last the five agreed, some with enthusiasm, others doubt-fully. And so it was decided that, as soon as the weather cleared, the barons would hasten northward to their baronies, like chaff blown before an oncoming storm, to harass Count Ulric's Army of the North when it sought passage through their property.

After the barons had retired for the night, Prospero asked Conan: 'Think you they will arrive in time?'

'For that matter,' added Trocero, 'will they hold true to their new alliance, if Numedides strews our path with steel or if Tarantia stands firm against us?'

Conan shrugged. 'I am no prophet. The gods alone can read the hearts of men.'

The sorcerer's chariot rumbled through the streets of Tarantia, with Hsiao, legs braced against the floorboards, gripping the reins and Thulandra Thuu in hooded cloak seated on the pillow-padded bench. Citizens who remarked the vehicle's approach turned away their faces. To meet the dark sorcerer's eyes might focus his attention, and all deemed it expedient to escape the magician's notice. For none there was who failed to hear rumours of his black experiments and tales of missing maidens.

The great bronze portals of the South Gate swung open at the vehicle's approach and closed behind it. Along the open country road, the strange steed paced at twice the speed of ordinary horseflesh, while the chariot bounced and swayed, trailing a thin plume of dust. More than forty leagues of white road unrolled with every passing day; and neither heat, nor rain, nor gloom of night stayed the iron stallion from its appointed task. When Hsiao wearied, his master grasped the reins. During these periods of rest, the yellow man devoured cold meats and snatched a spell of fitful sleep. Whether his master ever closed his eyes, Hsiao knew not.

After following the east bank of the River Khorotas for several days, Thulandra Thuu's chariot neared the great bridge that King Vilerus I had flung across the river. Here the Road of Kings, after swinging around two serpentine bends in the river, rejoined the stream and promptly crossed it to the western bank. The bridge, upraised on six stone piers that towered up from the river bed, was furnished with a wooden deck and a steeply sloping ramp on either end.

At the sight of the emblazoned chariot, the toll taker bowed low and waved the carriage through; and as the vehicle ascended to the deck, Thulandra scanned the countryside. When he perceived a cloud of dust, swirling aloft from the road ahead, a meagre smile of satisfaction creased his saturnine visage. If the pounding hooves of Prince Numitor's cavalry roiled the loose soil and bore it skyward, his careful calculations of time and distance had been correct. They would meet where the Bossonian Road conjoined with the highway to Poitain.

The chariot thundered down the western ramp and continued southward, and within the hour Thulandra overtook a column of horsemen. As the painted chariot neared, a trooper at the column's tail recognised the vehicle. When word ran up the ranks, the cavalrymen hastily pulled their mounts aside, leaving an unobstructed path for the royal sorcerer. The horses shied and danced as the black metallic steed sped past, and the milling remounts and frightened pack animals reared and plunged and much discomfited their handlers.

At the head of the column, the magician found Prince Numitor astride a massive gelding. Like his royal cousin the king, the prince was a man of heavy build, with a reddish tinge to hair and beard. Otherwise he presented quite a different aspect; guileless blue eyes graced a broad-browed, sun-browned face that bore the stamp of easy-going geniality.

'Why, Mage Thulandra!' exclaimed Numitor in amazement, when Hsiao reined in his singular steed. 'What brings you hither? Do you bear some urgent message from the king?'

'Prince Numitor, you will require my sorcerous arts to check the rebels' northward march.'

The prince's eyes clouded with perplexity. 'I like not magic in my warfare; it's not a manly way to fight. But if my royal cousin sent you, I must make the best of it.'

A glint of malice flared up in the sorcerer's hooded eyes. 'I speak for the true ruler of Aquilonia,' he said. 'And my commands must be obeyed. If we proceed with haste, we can reach the Imirian Escarpment before the rebels. Are these two regiments of horse all that you bring with you?'

'Nay, four regiments of foot follow. They have not yet reached the junction of the Bossonian Road with this.'

'None too many, although we face naught but a rabble of undisciplined rogues. If we can hold them below the cliff wall until Count Ulric arrives, we shall pluck their fangs. When we attain the crest of the escarpment, I wish you to detail five of your men – experienced hunters all – for a certain task.'

'What task is that, sir?'

'Of this I shall inform you later. Suffice it to say that skilled woodsmen are necessary to the spell I have in mind.'

At last the rain ceased in Culario. The northern barons and their entourage slogged along the muddy road, where vapour steamed from puddles drying in the summer sun. Shortly thereafter, the Army of Liberation set out upon the same highway, leading northward to the central provinces and thence to proud Tarantia on the far bank of the Khorotas.

At every town and hamlet that they passed, the legions of the Liberator were infused with new recruits: old knights, eager to take part in one last glorious affray; battle-battered ex-soldiers who had served with Conan on the Pictish frontier; lean foresters and huntsmen who saw in Conan a nature-lover like themselves; outlaws and exiles, drawn by the promise of amnesty for those who fought beneath the Golden Lion; yeomen, tradesmen and mechanics; wood-cutters, charcoal burners, smiths, masons, pavers, weavers, fullers, minstrels, clerks – all hard-eyed men eager to adventure in the army of the Liberator. They so drained the armoury of weapons that Conan at last insisted each recruit come already armed, if only with a woodsman's axe.

Conan and his officers plunged into the arduous task of welding these eager volunteers into some semblance of a military force. They told the men off into squads and companies and appointed sergeants and captains from those experienced in war. During halts, these new officers exercised their road-weary men in simple drills; for, as Conan warned them:

'Without constant practice, a horde of raw recruits like these dissolve into a mass of shrieking fugitives when the first blood is shed.'

Between the farm lands of southern Poitain and the Imirian Escarpment stretched the great Brocellian Forest, through which the highway glided like a serpent amid a bed of ferns. As the rebels neared the forest, the songs of the Poitanian volunteers diminished. More and more, Conan noted, the recruits tramped along in glum silence, apprehensively eyeing the overarching foliage.

'What ails them?' Conan asked Trocero as they sat of an evening in the command tent. 'Anyone would think these woods writhed with venomous serpents.'

The grey-haired count smiled indulgently. 'We have only

the common viper in Poitain, and few of those. But the folk hereabouts are full of peasant superstitions, holding the forest to harbour supernatural beings who may work magic on them. Such beliefs are not without advantage; they preserve a splendid hunting ground for my barons and my friends.'

Conan grunted. 'Once we scale the escarpment and gain the Imirian Plateau, they'll doubtless find some new hobgoblin to obsess them. I have not seen this part of Aquilonia before, but by my reckoning the cliff wall rises less than a day's march ahead. How runs the pass to the plateau?'

'There's a deep cleft in the cliff, where the turbulent Bitaxa River, a tributary of the Alimane, cascades across the wall of rock. The road, winding upward to the plateau, is borne upon a rock ledge thrust out from one side of the cleft. The gorge below – which we call the Giant's Notch – is slippery, steep, and narrow. An evil place to meet a cliff-top foe! Pray to your Crom that Numitor's Frontiersmen do not reach the Notch ahead of us.'

'Crom cares but little for the prayers of men,' said Conan, 'or so they told me when I was a boy. He breathes into each mortal man the strength to face his enemies; and that's all a man can reasonably ask of gods, who have their own concerns. But we must not risk attack in this murderous trap. Tomorrow at dawn, take a strong party of mounted scouts to reconnoitre the escarpment.'

Publius waddled in, arms full of ledgers, and Trocero left Conan studying the inventory of supplies. The count sought out the tents of his Poitanian horsemen and chose from amongst them forty skilled swordsmen for the morrow's reconnaissance.

The Giant's Notch loomed high above Trocero's company, its beetling cliffs hiding black wells of darkness from the midday sun. The count and his scouts sat their saddles, staring upward at the crest, searching in vain for the telltale sparkle of sunlight on armour. Neither could they observe upon the elevation the smoke of any campfires. At length Trocero said:

'We shall circle round the woods and meet again upon the road, a quarter-league back, where a high rock ledge overhangs the forest path. Vopisco, take your half of the detachment east and meet me thither within the hour. I shall go westward.'

The detachment divided, and the horsemen forced their mounts through the dense foliage that spilled out into the road. Once past this obstacle, they encountered little underbrush beneath the thick trunks of the virgin oaks.

For a short while Trocero's party rode in silence, their horses' hooves soundless on the thick carpet of mouldering leaves. Suddenly the forester in the lead flung up a hand, turned in his saddle, and murmured: 'Men ahead, my lord. Mounted, I think.'

The troop drew together, the men tense and apprehensive, their horses motionless. Through the shadowed ranks of trees Trocero's eyes detected a disquieting movement; his ears, a mutter of strange voices.

'Swords!' whispered the count. 'Prepare to charge, but strike not till I command. We know not whether they be friend or foe.'

Twenty swords hissed from their scabbards, as the riders eased their beasts to right or left, until they formed a line among the trees. The voices waxed louder, and a group of horsemen sprang into view beyond the rugged boles of immemorial oaks. His upraised sword a pointing finger, Trocero signalled the attack.

Weaving around the trees, the score of Poitanians rode at the strangers. In a few heartbeats they came within plain sight of them.

'Yield!' shouted Trocero, then reined his horse in blank amazement. The animal reared, eyes rolling, forelegs pawing the insubstantial air.

Five mounted men, unarmoured but wearing white surcoats adorned with the black eagle of Aquilonia, paused to stare. All but one led captive creatures by cruel ropes noosed tightly about their necks. The captives – three males and a female – were no larger than half-grown children, their nakedness partly veiled by a thin coat of fawnlike, light-brown fur. Above each snub-nosed, humanoid face rose a pair of pointed ears. When their captors dropped the leashing ropes to draw their swords, and the freed creatures turned to run, Trocero saw each bore a short, furry tail, like that of a deer, white on the underside.

The leader of the Aquilonians, recovering his composure, shouted an order to his men. Instantly, they spurred their mounts and charged.

'Kill them!' cried Trocero.

As the five royalists, bending low over their horses' necks, pounded towards the Poitanians, death rode in their grim eyes. The rebel swordsmen could not present a solid line, spread out as they were among the trees, so the Aquilonians aimed for the gaps. The leader rode at Trocero, his blade thrust outward like a lance. To right and left, the count's men, avenging furies, rushed headlong at the foe.

There was an instant of wild confusion, raked by shouts and illumined by the white light of terror in the eyes of men flogged by the fury of their desperation. Two troopers converged upon a galloping Aquilonian, whose upraised sword whirled murderously above his tousled head. One drove his steel into the soldier's sword arm; the other struck downward with all his might, tearing a long gash in the speeding horse's side. But the screaming animal pressed forward, and the man ran free.

A rebel's sword darted past a blade that sought to slash him and sheathed six inches of its point into an eagle-emblemed midriff. The lean, muscle-knotted Aquilonian leader lunged at Trocero, who parried with a clang, and the hum of steel on steel was a song of death. Then the five horses were through and away, like autumn leaves in a gale, with four of their riders. The fifth lay supine on the leaf mould of the forest floor, with a bloodstain spreading slowly across his white surcoat.

'Gremio!' shouted the count. 'Take your squad and pursue! Try to capture one alive!'

Trocero turned back to the trampled turf, which bore mute testimony to the furious encounter. Spying the fallen man, he said: 'Sergeant, see if that fellow lives.'

As the sergeant dismounted, another trooper said: 'Please, my lord, he spitted himself on my steel as he rode past. I know he's dead.'

'He is,' nodded the sergeant, after a quick examination.

Trocero cursed. 'We needed him for questioning!'

'Here's one of their captives,' said the sergeant, kneeling beside the nude creature, flung like a discarded garment against a fallen log. 'Me thinks it was knocked down by a flying hoof and stunned in the mêlée.'

Trocero bit his underlip in thought. 'It is, I do believe, a fabled satyr, whereof the countryfolk tell fearsome old-wives' tales.'

A look of superstitious terror crossed the sergeant's face, and he snatched back his questing hands. 'What shall I do with it, sir,' he said, rising and stepping backward.

The satyr, whose wrists were bound together by a narrow thong, opened its eyes, perceived the ring of hostile mounted men, and scrambled to its feet. Trembling, it sought to run; but the sergeant, grabbing the rope that trailed from its neck, tugged and brought it down.

When it had been subdued, Trocero addressed it: 'Creature, can you talk?'

'Aye,' the captive said in broken Aquilonian. 'Talk good. Talk my tongue; talk little yours. What you do to me?'

'That's for our general to decide,' replied Trocero.

'You no cut throat, like other men?'

'I have no wish to cut your throat. Why think you that those others so would do?'

'Others catch us for magic sacrifice.'

The count grunted. 'I see. You need fear naught of that from us. But we must bring you back to camp. Have you a name?'

'Me Gola,' said the satyr in his gentle voice.

'Then, Gola, you shall ride pillion behind one of my men. Do you understand?'

The satyr looked downcast. 'Me fear horse.'

'You must overcome your fear,' said Trocero, giving his sergeant a signal.

'Up you go,' said the soldier, swinging the small form aloft; and, lifting the noose from Gola's neck, he bound the rope firmly about the satyr's waist and that of the trooper on whose horse the creature sat.

'You'll be quite safe,' he laughed. Swinging into his saddle, he turned the column around.

The squad sent in pursuit of the royalists arrived at the base of the Giant's Notch in time to see the fugitives disappear up the steep tunnel of the gorge. Fearing ambush, the Poitanians pressed the pursuit no further.

Later, in the command tent, Trocero reported on his mission to the assembled leaders of the rebellion. Conan surveyed the captive and said: 'That binding on your wrists seems tight, friend Gola. We need it not.'

He drew his dagger and approached the satyr, who cringed and screamed in mortal terror: 'No cut throat! Man promise, no cut throat!'

'Forget your precious throat!' growled Conan, seizing the captive's wrists in one gigantic hand. 'I would not harm you.' He slashed the thong and sheathed his poinard, while Gola flexed his fingers and winced at the pain of returning circulation.

'That's better, eh?' said Conan, seating himself at the trestle table and beckoning the satyr to join him. 'Do you like wine, Gola?'

The satyr smiled and nodded; and Conan signalled to his squire.

'General!' exclaimed Publius, holding up a finger to stay the execution of the order. 'Our wine is nearly gone. A few flagons more and we're all back on beer.'

'No matter,' said Conan. 'Wine we shall have. The

Nemedians have a saying, "In wine is truth", and this I am about to test.'

Publius, Trocero and Prospero exchanged glances. Since he first clapped eyes upon the satyr, Conan displayed a curious affinity for this subhuman being. It was as if, a scarce-tamed creature of the wild himself, he felt instinctive sympathy for another child of nature, dragged from its native haunts by civilised men whose ways and motives must be utterly incomprehensible.

Half a wineskin later, Conan discovered that two regiments of royalist cavalry held the plateau above the Imirian Escarpment. They were encamped, not at the cliff-top where they could attack if the rebels ascended the flume of the Giant's Notch, but several bowshots – perhaps a quarter-league – back from the edge. And for several days royalist hunting parties had clambered down the Notch to sweep the neighbouring woods for satyrs. Those they caught, they dragged alive back to their camp and penned them, still bound, in a stockade built for the purpose.

'My folk move from Notch,' said Gola, sadly. 'Had no pipes ready.'

Ignoring that strange remark, Conan asked: 'How know you that they plan to use your people's blood for magical sacrifices?'

The satyr gave Conan a sly, sidelong glance. 'We know. We, too, have magic. Big magician on cliffs above.'

Conan pondered, studying the small creature intently. 'Gola, if we push the bad men from the upper plain, you need no longer fear mistreatment. If you help us, we will restore your woods to you.'

'How know I what big men do? Big men kill our people.'

'Nay, we are your friends. See, you are free to go.' Conan pointed to the tent flap, arms spread wide.

A glow of childlike joy suffused the satyr's face. Conan waited for the glow to fade, then said: 'Now that we've saved some of your folk from the wizard's cauldron, we may ask help from you. How can I reach you?'

Gola showed Conan a small tube made of bone that was suspended from a vine entwined about his neck. 'Go in woods and blow.' The satyr put the whistle to his lips and puffed his cheeks.

'I hear no sound,' said Conan.

'Nay, but satyr hear. You take.'

Conan stared at the tiny whistle as it lay in his huge palm. while the others frowned, thinking the bit of bone a useless toy intended to cozen their general. Presently, Conan slipped the whistle into his pouch, saying gravely: 'I thank you, little friend.' Then calling his squires and the nearest sentry, he said: 'Escort Gola into the woods beyond the camp. Let none molest him – some of our superstitious soldiers might deem him an embodied evil spirit and take a cut at him. Farewell.'

When the satyr had departed, Conan addressed his comrades: 'Numitor lies beyond the Notch, waiting for us to climb the slope ere he signals attack! What make you of it?'

Prospero shrugged. 'Meseems he relies much on that "big magician" – the king's sorcerer, I have no doubt.'

Trocero shook his head. 'More likely, he's fain to give us a clear path to the top, so that we can face him on equal terms. He is a well-meaning gentleman who thinks to fight a war by rules of chivalry.'

'He must know we outnumber him,' said Publius, perplexed.

'Aye,' retorted Trocero, 'but his troops are Aquilonia's best, whereas half our motley horde are babes playing at warfare. So he relies on dash and discipline . . .'

The argument was long and inconclusive. As twilight deepened into night, Conan banged his goblet on the table. 'We cannot sit below the cliffs for ay, attempting to read Numitor's mind. Tomorrow we shall scale the Giant's Notch, prepared for instant action.'

X

Satyrs' Blood

Prince Numitor paced restlessly about the royalist camp.
The cooking fires were dying down, and the regiments of
Royal Frontiersmen had turned in for the night. The new
moon set, and in the gathering darkness the stars wheeled
slowly westward like diamonds stitched upon the night-blue
cloak of a dancing girl. To the west, where twilight lingered,
the dodging shape of a foraging bat besmudged the horizon,
while overhead the clap of a nightjar's wings shattered the
silence.

The prince passed the line of sentries and strolled towards
the edge of the escarpment, where Thulandra Thuu had
placed things needful for his magic. Behind him the camp
vanished into forest-shadowed darkness. Ahead the precipice
fell sharply away. And leftward yawned the black canyon
that was called the Giant's Notch.

Although the prince's placid ears picked up no sound of
movement in the gorge, something about the camp's location
disturbed him; but for a time he could not put a finger on
the source of his unease.

After walking several bowshots' distance, Prince Numitor
sighted the dancing flames of a small fire. He hastened
towards it. Thulandra Thuu, hooded and cloaked in black,
like some bird of ill omen, was bending over the fire, while
Hsiao, on his knees, fed the blaze with twigs. A metal tripod,
from the apex of which a small brazen pot was suspended
by a chain, straddled the fickle fire. To one side a large copper
cauldron squatted in the grass.

As Numitor approached, the sorcerer moved away from
the firelight and, fumbling in a leathern wallet, extracted a
crystal phial. This he unstoppered, muttering an incantation

in an unknown tongue, and poured the contents into the heated vessel. A sudden hissing and a plume of smoke, shot through with rainbow hues, issued from the pot.

Thulandra Thuu glanced at the prince, said a brief 'Good even, my lord!' and reached again into his wallet.

'Master Thulandra!' said Numitor.

'Sir?' The sorcerer paused in his searching.

'You insisted that the camp be set far from the precipice; I wonder at your reasoning. Should the rebels steal into the Giant's Notch, they would be upon us ere they were discovered. Why not move the camp here on the morrow, where our men can readily assail the foe with missiles from above?'

The eyes beneath the sorcerer's cowl were veiled in purple darkness, but the prince fancied that they glowed deep in that cavernous hollow, like the night eyes of beasts of prey. Thulandra purred: 'My lord Prince, if the demons I unleash perform their proper function, my spell would put your men in danger should they stand where we stand now. The final stage I shall commence at midnight, a scant three hours hence. Hsiao will inform you in good time.'

The magician shook more powder into the steaming pot and stirred the molten mixture with a slender silver rod. 'Now I crave your pardon, good my lord, but I must ask you to stand back whilst I construct my pentacle.'

Hsiao handed Thulandra Thuu the wooden staff, ornately carved, which served him as a walking stick when he stalked about the camp. While his servant piled fresh fuel upon the dying fire, the sorcerer paced off certain distances about the conflagration and marked the bare earth with the ferule of his staff. Muttering, he drew a circle, a dozen paces in diameter, then etched deep lines back and forth across the space enclosed. Following an arcane ritual, he inscribed a symbol in each angle of the pentacle. The prince understood neither the diagram nor the lettering thereon, but felt no desire to plumb the wizard's unholy mysteries.

Now Thulandra rose up and stood beside his fire, his back to the precipice. He intoned an utterance – a prayer or incantation – in a singsong foreign tongue. Then, facing east, he repeated his invocation, and in this wise completed one rotation. Numitor saw the stars grow dim and shapeless shadows flutter through the clear night air. He heard the sinister thunder of unseen beating wings. Thinking it better not to view more of the uncanny preparations of his cousin's favourite, he stumbled back to camp. To his captains he gave orders to rouse the men an hour before midnight to comply with the sorcerer's directions. Then he turned in.

Three hours later Hsiao spoke to a sentry, who sent another to awaken the sleeping prince. As Numitor made his way to the cliff whereon the wizard prepared his magical spell, he came upon the column of soldiers ordered by Thulandra Thuu. Each man-at-arms gripped a bound and captive satyr. A dozen of the furry forest folk whimpered and wailed as their captors brutally hustled them into line.

Hsiao had built up the fire, and the brazen pot bubbled merrily, sending a cloud of varicoloured smoke into the star-lit sky. Upon Thulandra's curt command, the first soldier in the line dragged his squirming captive to the copper cauldron standing upon the grass and forced the bleating creature's head down over the vessel's rim. As the darkness throbbed to the beat of an inaudible drum – or was it the beat of the awestruck soldiers' hearts? – the sorcerer deftly slashed the satyr's throat. At a signal, the man-at-arms lifted the sacrificial victim by its ankles and drained its blood into the large container. Then, in obedience to a low command, he tossed the small cadaver over the precipice.

A pause ensued while Thulandra added more powders to his sinister brew and pronounced another incantation. At length he beckoned to the next man in line, who dragged his satyr forward to be slain. The other soldiers shifted uneasy feet. One muttered:

'This takes longer than a coronation! Would he'd get on with it and let us back to bed.'

The eastern sky was paling when the last satyr died. The fire beneath the brazen pot had burned to a bed of embers. Hsiao, at his master's command, unhooked the steaming pot and poured its boiling contents into the blood-filled cauldron.

The nearest soldiers saw – or thought they saw – ghostly forms rise from the latter vessel; but others perceived only great clouds of vapour. In the deceptive predawn half-light, none could be sure of what he saw.

Faintly in the distance those on the cliff-top heard the sound of men in motion. Among the marching men no word was spoken, but the jingle of harness and the tramp of many feet cried defiance to the silent morning air.

Thulandra Thuu raised a voice shrill with tension: 'My lord! Prince Numitor! Order your men away!'

Startled out of his sleepy lethargy, the prince barked the command: 'Stand to arms! Back to camp!'

The sounds of an approaching army grew. The sorcerer raised his arms and droned an invocation. Hsiao handed him a dipper, with which he scooped up liquid from the cauldron and poured the fluid into a deep crack in the rocks. He stepped back, raised imploring arms against the lightening sky, and cried out again in unknown tongues. Then he ladled out another dipperful, and another.

Along the road from Culario, before that sandy ribbon disappeared beneath a canopy of leaves, the mage could see a pair of mounted men. They trotted towards the Giant's Notch, and as they went they studied the rock wall and the woods below it. Then a whole troop of cavalry came into view; and following them, files of infantry, swinging along with weapons balanced on their shoulders.

Thulandra Thuu hastily ladled out more liquid from the cauldron and once more raised his skinny arms to heaven.

Leading the first rank of rebel horse, Conan rose in his stirrups to peer about. His scouts had seen no royalists in the greenery along the forest road, or at the Giant's Notch, or atop the towering cliffs. The Cimmerian's eagle glance raked the summit, now tipped a rosy pink by the slanting rays of the morning sun. Conan's apprehension of hidden traps stirred in his savage soul. Prince Numitor was no genius, this he knew; but even such a one as he would make ready to defend the Notch.

Yet he saw no sign of a royalist mustering. Would Numitor, indeed, allow the rebels to reach the Imirian Plateau to lessen the odds against them? Conan knew the nobles of this land professed obedience to the rules of chivalry; but in all his years of war, no general had ever risked a certain chance of victory for such an abstract principle. Nay, the enemy had the upper hand; a trap was obvious! Experience with the hypocrisies of civilised men made the Cimmerian cynical about the ideals they so eloquently proclaimed. The barbarians among whom he had grown to manhood were quite as treacherous; but they did not seek to gild their bloody actions with noble sentiments.

One scout reported a strange discovery. At the base of the escarpment, leftward of the Giant's Notch, he had come upon a heap of satyr corpses, each with its throat ripped open. The bodies, smashed and scattered, had fallen from the heights above.

'Sorcery afoot!' muttered Trocero. 'The king's he-witch has joined with Numitor, I'll wager.'

As the two lead horsemen neared the Notch, they spurred their steeds and vanished up the road that paralleled the turgid River Bitaxa. Soon they reappeared upon a rocky ledge and signalled all was quiet. Conan scanned the summit once again. He thought he caught a hint of movement – a mere black speck that might have been a trick of light or of tired eyes. Turning, he motioned the leader of the troop, Captain Morenus, to enter the tunnel of the Notch.

Conan sat his mount beside the road, watching intently. As the horsemen trotted past, his heart swelled at the soldierly appearance they made, thanks to the driving force of his incessant drilling. His own horse, a bay gelding, seemed restless, stamping its hooves and dancing sideways. Conan stroked the creature's neck to gentle it, but the bay continued to fidget. He first thought the animal was impatient to move forward with the others of the troop; but as the horse became more agitated, a premonition took shape in Conan's mind.

After another glance at the escarpment Conan, a scowl

on his scarred face, swung off his beast and dropped with a clash of armour to the ground. Gripping his reins, he shut his eyes. His barbarian senses, keener than those of city-bred men, had not deceived him. Through the soles of his boots he felt a faint quivering in the earth. Not the vibration that a group of galloping horsemen sends through the ground, this was something slower, more deliberate, with more actual motion, as if the earth had waked to yawn and stretch.

Conan hesitated no longer. Cupping his hands around his mouth and filling his great lungs, he bellowed: 'Morenus, come back! Get out of the Notch! Spur your horses, all! Come back!'

There was a moment of confusion in the Notch, as the command was passed along and the soldiers sought to turn their steeds on the narrow way. Above them on the cliff, the sorcerer shrieked a final invocation and struck the rocks outside his pentacle with his curiously carven staff.

A rumble – a deep-toned roll that scarcely could be heard – issued from the earth. Above the retreating cavalrymen, the cliffs swayed. Pieces of black basalt detached themselves and toppled, with deceptive slowness, then faster and faster, striking ledges, shattering, and bounding off to crash into the gorge. From the River Bitaxa, towering jets of spray fountained aloft to dwarf the downward fall of the cascade.

Conan found his stirrup with some difficulty, as his terror-stricken beast danced around him in a circle. His foot secured, he swung cursing into the saddle and wheeled to face the column of infantry, still marching briskly towards the Notch.

'Get back! Get back!' he roared, but his words were lost in the grumbling, grinding thunder of the earthquake. He moved his horse into the column's path, making frantic gestures. The lead men understood and checked their gait; but those behind continued to press forward, so that the column bunched up into a milling mass.

Within the Notch the cliffs swayed, reeled, and crumbled. With the roar of an angry god, millions of tons of rock cascaded into the gap. The earth beneath the soldiers' feet so swayed and bounced that men clutched one another to stay erect; a few fell, their weapons clattering to the rocky ground.

Down from the deadly flume raced Conan's troop of cavalry, lashed by their panic. The leaders crashed into the infantry column, downing some horses, spilling riders from their saddles, and injuring many foot soldiers caught in the pincer's jaws. Men's shouts and horses' screams soared above the thunder of the 'quake.

The Bitaxa River foamed out of its bed, as waves sent downstream by the fall of rock spread out on the flatlands below and lapped across the road. Soldiers splashed ankle-deep in water and prayed to their assorted gods.

Controlling his frantic mount by a savage grip on the reins, Conan sought to restore order. 'Morenus!' he shouted. 'Did all your men get out?'

'All but a dozen or so in the van, General.'

Glowering at the Giant's Notch, Conan cursed the loss. A vast cloud of dust obscured the pass, until a wind sprang up and swept it out. As the dust thinned, Conan saw that the Notch was now much wider than before and that its slopes were less than vertical. The flume was filled with a huge talus of broken rock – stones of all sizes, from pebbles to fragments as large as a tent. From time to time small slides continued to issue from the sloping walls and clatter down upon the talus. Any man caught beneath that fall of rock would be entombed forever.

One section to the left side of the cliff had curiously remained in place; it now rose from the slope like a narrow buttress. At the pinnacle of this strange formation, Conan saw a pair of small figures, black-robed and cowled. One tossed its arms on high, as if in supplication.

'That's the king's sorcerer, Thulandra Thuu, or I'm a Stygian!' rasped a voice nearby.

Conan turned to see Gromel at his elbow. 'Think you he sent the earthquake?'

'Aye. And if he'd waited till we were all within the Notch, we'd all be dead. He's too far for a bowshot; but if I had a bow, I'd chance it.'

An archer heard and handed up his bow, saying: 'Try mine, sir!'

Gromel dismounted, drew an arrow to the head, shifted aim by a hair's breadth, and let fly. The arrow arced high and struck the cliff a score of paces below the top. The small figures vanished.

'A good try,' grunted Conan. 'We should have set up a ballista. Gromel, there are broken bones in need of splints; see that the physicians do their work.'

Under lowering brows Conan stared at the talus. His barbarian instincts told him to rally his men, dismount the cavalry, and lead them all in a headlong charge up the steep incline, leaping from rock to rock with naked steel in hand. But experience warned him that this would be a futile gesture, throwing away men's lives to no good purpose. Progress would be slow and laborious; the struggling climbers would be raked by arrows from above; those who survived the climb would be too winded to do battle.

He looked around. 'Ho there, Trocero! Prospero! Morenus, send a trooper to tell Publius and Pallantides that I want them here. Now, friends, what next?'

Count Trocero reined his horse closer to Conan's and studied the mass of broken rock. 'The army can in no way ascend the slope. Men afoot might slowly pick their way up – if Numitor did not assail them and the sorcerer cast no other deadly spell. But horses never, nor yet the wains.'

'Could we build our own road, replacing the rock-ledge path that lies beneath the rocks?' suggested Prospero.

Trocero considered the idea. 'With a thousand workmen, several months, and gold to spare, I'd build you as fine a road as you could wish.'

'We do not have such time, nor money either,' rumbled Conan. 'If we cannot go through the Notch, we must go over, under, or around it. Order the men to march a quarter-league back along the road and pitch camp under the forest trees.'

In the royalist camp Thulandra Thuu confronted a furious

prince. The exhausted sorcerer, looking much older than was his wont, leaned on Hsiao's sturdy shoulder. The area on which his pentacle was marked had not fallen with the balance of the cliff, and he had walked the narrow bridge to safety.

'You fool necromancer!' grumbled Numitor. 'Since you would resort to magic, you should have waited till the Notch was filled with rebels. Thus we had slain them all. Now they have fled with little scathe.'

'You do not understand these matters, Prince,' replied Thulandra coolly. 'I withheld the final step of the enchantment until I saw that something – or someone – had warned the rebel leader of the trap and the rebels had begun to flee. Had I withheld my hand the longer, they would have all escaped scot-free. In any case the flume is blocked. The rebels must needs march east to the Khorotas or west to the Alimane, for they cannot now breach the escarpment.

'And now Your Highness must excuse me. The spell has drained my psychic forces, and I must rest.'

'I never did think much of miracle-mongers,' growled Numitor as he turned away.

In the sheltered forest camp that evening, Conan and his officers reviewed a map. 'To bypass the escarpment,' said Conan, 'we must return to the village of Pedassa, whence the roads depart for the two rivers. But that's a lengthy march.'

'If there were some little-known break in the long cliff wall,' said Prospero wistfully, 'we could, by moving quietly through the woods, steal a march on Numitor and fall upon him unawares.'

Conan frowned. 'This map shows no such pass; but long ago I learned not to trust mapmakers. You're lucky if they show the rivers flowing in the true direction. Trocero, know you any alternate route?'

Trocero shook his head. 'Nay.'

'There must be streams other than the Bitaxa that cut a channel in the cliff.'

Trocero shrugged helplessly. Pallantides entered, saying:

'Your pardon, General, but two men of Serdicus's company have deserted.'

Conan snorted. 'Every time we win, men desert from the royalists to join us; every time we lose, they desert us for the king. It is like a game of chance, following Fate's decree. Send scouts to look for them and hang them if you catch them; but do not make a public matter of it. Order woodsmen at dawn to study the cliff face in both directions for the distance of a league to see if they can find a pathway to the top. And now, friends, leave me to ponder further on the matter.'

Beside his camp bed Conan brooded over a flagon of ale. He restudied the map and cudgelled his brain for a way his army might surmount the escarpment.

Absently he fingered the half-circle of obsidian, which once had hung between the opulent breasts of tl.e dancing girl Alcina, and which was now clasped around his massive neck. He stared down at the object, thinking how right had been his friend Trocero's suspicion that she had caused the death of old Amulius Procas.

Little by little, the pieces of the puzzle fitted together. Alcina had been sent – either by the king's spymaster or by the royal sorcerer – to try to murder him. Later she succeeded in slaying General Procas. Why Procas? Because with Conan in his grave, Procas was no longer needed to defend Aquilonia's mad king. Hence, neither she nor her master knew, at the time of Procas's death, that Conan had recovered from her deadly elixir.

Well, thought Conan, not without bitterness, he must hereafter be more cautious in choosing his bedmates. But why should Procas die? Because Alcina's master, whoever he might be, wanted the old man out of his way. This thought led Conan to Thulandra Thuu, for the rivalry between the sorcerer and the general for the king's favour was notorious.

Conan gripped the ebon talisman as this enlightenment burst upon him. And as he did so, he became aware of a curious sensation. It seemed that voices carried on a dialogue within his skull.

A shadowy form took shape before his eyes. As Conan tensed to snatch his sword, the vision solidified, and he saw a female figure sitting on a black wrought-iron throne. The vision was to some extent transparent – Conan could dimly see the tent wall behind the image – and too nebulous to recognise the woman's features. But in the shadowy face burned eyes of emerald green.

With every nerve atingle, Conan watched the figure and harkened to the voices. One was a woman's dusky voice, and her words followed the movements of the shadow's lips. The voice was Alcina's, but she seemed unaware of Conan's scrutiny.

The other voice was dry, metallic, passionless, and spoke Aquilonian with a sibilant slur. Conan had never exchanged a word with Thulandra Thuu, although he had seen the mage across the throne room during courtly functions in Tarantia when he was general to the king. But from descriptions of the wizard, he imagined the king's favourite would speak thus. The voice proceeded:

'. . . I know not who betrayed my plan; but some treacher must have forewarned the rebel chieftain.'

Alcina replied: 'Perhaps not, Master. The barbarian pig has senses keener than those of ordinary men; he might have detected the coming cataclysm by some stirring of the air above the earth. What do you now?'

'I must needs remain here to guard that ninny Numitor against some asinine misjudgement, until Count Ulric arrives. The stars inform me of his coming in three days' time. Yet I am weary. Calling up the spirits of the earth has prostrated me. I can work no further spells until I recoup my psychic forces.'

'Then, pray, come back forthwith!' urged the vision of Alcina. 'Ulric will surely arrive before the rebels can surmount the cliffs, and I have need of your protection.'

'Protection? Why so?'

'His maggotty Majesty, the King, importunes me constantly to join him in his bestial amusements. I am afraid.'

'What has this walking heap of excrement been urging you to do?'

'His desires beggar all description, Master. At your command, some men I have lain with, and some I have slain. But this I will not do.'

'Set and Kali!' exclaimed the dry male voice. 'When I have finished with Numedides, he'll wish he were in hell! I shall set forth for Tarantia on the morrow.'

'Have a care that you fall not into rebel hands along the way! Insurgent bands have been reported along the Road of Kings, and the barbarian pig might lead a swift raid into loyal territory. He is a worthy adversary.'

The male voice chuckled faintly. 'Fear not for me, my dear Alcina. Even in my present depleted state, I can with my peculiar powers slay any mortal at close quarters. And now, farewell.'

The voices fell silent, and the vision faded. Conan shook himself like one awakening from a vivid dream. With Thulandra gone from the scene of battle and Ulric not yet arrived, he had a chance to fall on Numitor's army and rout it – if only he could reach the plains above before the Count of Raman came with reinforcements.

He needed air to clear his rampant thoughts and rose to leave his narrow sleeping quarters. In the adjacent section of the tent, the bodyguards whom Prospero had assigned him were so engrossed in a game of chance that none looked up as Conan, soundless as a shadow, glided past them.

Outside, the sentries, used to his night prowls, supposed that he was making an inspection. They saluted as he wandered to the edge of the encampment and continued into the nighted woods. Prospero, he thought with a grim smile, would be perturbed to know that Conan once again had given his bodyguards the slip.

He fumbled in his wallet for the bone whistle Gola had given him, retrieved it, and fingered it. The satyr had said that if he ever wanted help from the people of these woods, he had but to blow upon it. Half in jest, he put the tiny whistle to his lips and blew. Nothing happened. More urgently, he blew another silent blast.

Perhaps the remnant of the satyrs had departed from the scene of their destruction. Even if they heard the call, they might need time to come to him. Conan stood motionless with the wary patience of a crouching panther waiting for its prey, listening to the buzz and chirp of insects and the rustle of a passing breeze. Now and then he put the soundless whistle to his lips and blew again.

At length he felt a movement in the shrubbery. 'Who you, blow whistle call satyr?' asked a small high-pitched voice in broken Aquilonian.

'Gola?'

'Nay, me Zudik, chief. Who you?' The shrubbery parted.

'Conan the Cimmerian. Do you know Gola?' Conan, whose eyes had adjusted to the darkness, could see this was a bent and ancient satyr, whose pelt was tinged with silver.

'Aye,' replied the satyr chieftain. 'He tell about you. Save him and four others. What you want?'

'Your help to kill the men atop the cliff.'

'How Zudik help big man like you?'

'We need a pathway to the top,' said Conan, 'now that the Giant's Notch is filled with rocks. Know you another way?'

The night sang with the sound of insects in the silence. Then Zudik answered slowly: 'Is small path that way.' The satyr pointed eastward.

'How far?'

The satyr replied in his own language, and his words were like the caws of crows.

Puzzled, the Cimmerian asked: 'Can we get there within a day's march?'

'Walk hard. Can do.'

'Will you show us the way?'

'Aye. Be ready before sun-up.'

Later Conan sought out Publius and said: 'We move at dawn for a path the satyrs say leads to the bluff; but it's too narrow for the wagons. You will take the baggage train back to Pedassa and follow the road thence to the Khorotas. If we join you on the road to Tarantia, we shall have vanquished Numitor; if not –' Conan drew a finger across his throat – 'you'll go alone.'

The second gap in the escarpment was much narrower than the Giant's Notch. From below it was invisible, hidden by lush greenery and overhanging rocks. The horsemen had to lead their mounts across the brook that gurgled at the bottom of the cleft and up the rocky way. More than one horse, frightened by the narrowing canyon walls, held up the others while it whinnied, rolled frightened eyes, and reared.

The men afoot, walking in single file, could just squeeze through. When dusk made the path darker and more sinister, Conan urged each man to grasp the garments of the man ahead and stumble forward. Morning saw the last man through.

While the Army of Liberation rested from their forced march and arduous climb, Conan sent scouts to probe Numitor's position. On their return the leader reported:

'Numitor has struck his camp and fallen back for several leagues along the road. His men have pitched camp in the forest, straddling the highway.'

Conan looked a question at his officers. Pallantides said: 'What's this? Even if Numitor is stupid, I've never heard he was a coward!'

'More likely,' Trocero put in, 'he learned that we have found a way up the escarpment and feared we would drive him to the precipice.'

'The sorcerer might have warned him,' ventured Prospero.

'That is not all, General,' said the chief scout. 'Four more regiments have arrived to reinforce the enemy. We recognised their banners.'

Conan grunted. 'Numitor has stripped the Westermarck of regulars, leaving the defence against the Picts to the local militia. So we are again outnumbered; and the Royal Frontiersmen are skilful fighting men. I've fought beside them and I know.' He paused a moment, then added: 'Friends, that satyr Gola said something about using pipes against a foe. What think you that he meant?'

None knew. At last Conan said: 'I see I must consult our little folk again.'

As dusk drew a grey veil of mist along the tumbling stream, Conan worked his way down the narrow path up which his men had so laboriously clambered. He stood alone in the enshrouding dark of the Brocellian Forest, listening in vain for any footfall. He blew on the bone whistle and, as before, he waited in the shadow of an ancient tree. When at last his call was answered, he was relieved to find it was Zudik, the satyr who had directed his army to the pass. In answer to a question, Zudik said:

'Aye, we use pipes. Make your men stop up ears.'

'Plug up our ears?' asked Conan wonderingly.

'Aye. Use beeswax, cloth, clay – so can no longer hear. Then we help you.'

Numitor's Frontiersmen lay in a crescent across the highway to Tarantia. The prince seemed prepared to stand on the defensive until the arrival of Count Ulric. His men were digging earthworks with implanted pointed stakes to impede an attacker. Because of the dense stands of trees, the rebels could not outflank the royalists's long line.

Silently, the Army of Liberation spread out before the crescent, their presence hidden by the shrubbery. But when a royal sentry perceived a movement in the bushes, he sounded an alarm. Men dropped their shovels, snatched weapons, and took positions on the line.

Conan signalled to his aides, whose ears were plugged, to tell the archers to ply the foe with arrows; and presently, the thrum of bowstrings and the whistle of arrows rent the air. But Conan's men heard nothing.

To the royalist defenders on the ends of the line came a chilling sound – a shrill, ululating, unearthly piping. It came from nowhere into everywhere. It made men's teeth ache and imbued them with a strange, unreasoning panic. Soldiers dropped their weapons to clutch at pain-racked heads. Some burst into hysterical laughter; others dissolved in tears.

As the sound drew nearer, the feeling of dire doom expanded until it overflowed their souls. The impulse to be gone, which at first they mastered, overcame their years of battle training. Here and there a man turned from his position on the line to run, screaming madly, to the rear. More joined the flight, until the outer limits of the line dissolved into a mass of terrified fugitives, running from they knew not what. As the prince's flanks were swept away, the unseen pipers moved towards the centre, until that, too, disintegrated. Trocero's cavalry rode down the fleeing men, slaying and taking prisoners.

'Anyway,' said Conan as he looked at the abandoned royalist camp, 'they left us weapons enough for twice our number. So now we can recruit whatever volunteers we find.'

'That was an easy victory,' exulted Prospero.

'Too easy,' replied Conan grimly. 'An easy victory is oft as false as a courtier's smile. I'll say the road to Tarantia is open when I see the city walls, and not before.'

XI

The Key to the City

The Army of Liberation tramped unopposed through the smiling land, where Poitain's herds of fine horses and cattle grazed on luxuriant grass, and castles reared their crenelated towers of crimson and purple and gold. The rebel army serpentined its way through pillow-rounded mountains, lush with vegetation, and at last approached the border between Poitain and the central provinces of Aquilonia.

But as Conan sat his charger on an embankment to watch his soldiers pass before him, his gaze was sombre. For, although Numitor's Frontiersmen had scattered like leaves in an autumn gale, a new foe, against which he had no defence, now assailed his army. This was sickness. A malady, which caused men to break out in scarlet spots and prostrated them with chills and fever, raced through his ranks, an invisible demon, felling more soldiers than a hard-fought battle. Many men were left abed in villages along the way; many, fearing the dread disease, deserted; many died.

'What do we number now?' Conan asked Publius of an evening, as the army neared the border village of Elymia.

The former chancellor studied his reports. 'About eight thousand, counting the walking sick, who number nigh a thousand.'

'Crom! We were ten thousand when we left the Alimane, and hundreds more have joined since then. What has become of them?'

Trocero said: 'Some come to us in a roseate glow, like a bridegroom to his bride, but think better of their bargain when they have sweated and slogged a few leagues from their native heath. They fret about their families and getting home to harvest.'

'And this spotted sickness has claimed thousands,' added Dexitheus. 'I, and the physicians under me, have tried every herb and purge to no avail. It seems magic is at work. Else an evil destiny doth shape our ends.'

Conan bit back scornful words of incredulity. After the earthquake he dared not underestimate the potent magic of his enemy or the wanton cruelty of the gods.

'Could we have persuaded the satyrs to march with us, bringing their pipes,' said Prospero, 'our paltry numbers would be of little moment.'

'But they would not leave their homes in the Brocellian Forest,' said Conan.

Prospero replied: 'You could have seized their old Zudik as a hostage, to compel them.'

'That's not my way,' growled Conan. 'Zudik proved a friend in need. I would not use him ill.'

Trocero smiled gently. 'And are you not the man who scorned Prince Numitor for his high-flown ideals of chivalry?'

Conan grunted. 'With savages, the chief has little power; I have dwelt amongst them, and I know. Besides, I doubt if even great love for their chieftain's weal would overcome the little people's fear of open country. But let us face the future and not raise ghosts from the dead past. Have the scouts reported signs of Ulric's army?'

'No reports,' said Trocero, 'save that today they glimpsed a few riders from afar, who quickly galloped out of sight. We know not who they are; but I would wager that the northern barons delay Count Ulric still.'

'Tomorrow,' said Conan, 'I shall take Gyrto's troop to scout the border of Poitain, whilst the rest march for Elymia.'

'General,' objected Prospero. 'You should not use yourself so recklessly. A commander should stay behind the lines, where he can control his units, and not risk his life like a landless adventurer.'

Conan frowned. 'If I am commander here, I must command as I think best!' Seeing Prospero's stricken face, he added with a smile: 'Fear not; I'll do naught foolish. But even a general must betimes share the dangers of his men. Besides, am I not myself a landless adventurer?'

'Methinks,' grumbled Prospero, 'you merely indulge your barbarian lust for combat hand-to-hand.' Conan's grin widened wolfishly, but he ignored the comment.

The road was a golden ribbon before them, as Conan's troop trotted through the misty morning. At the column's head rode Conan, clad in chain mail like the others, and Captain Gyrto rode at his side. With lance fixed into a stirrup boot, each cavalryman rode proudly through the rolling country-side. A few detached outriders cantered in wide circles across the fallow fields but skirted the simple farmsteads and the stands of ripening grain.

Rustics at work on furrow or vine paused in their labours to lean on rake or hoe and stare, as the armed men rode past. One or two raised a cautious cheer, but most remained stolidly noncommittal and silent. Now and then Conan caught a flash of red or yellow petticoat, as a woman rushed to hide herself from the passing soldiery.

'They wait to see who wins,' said Gyrto.

'And well they might,' said Conan, 'for, if we lose, all who aided us will suffer for it.'

Beyond the next rise, Elymia squatted in a shallow vale. A small stream meandered sluggishly past the mud-brick houses, wending its way eastward towards the Khorotas, while willows contemplated their reflections in the dark, slow-moving water.

The village, which sheltered less than two hundred souls, lacked protection; for decades of peace had so beguiled the villagers that they allowed the old wall of sun-dried brick to crumble utterly. Inhabitants – if any there were who laboured in the hamlet – were nowhere to be seen.

'It's too quiet for me,' muttered Conan. 'People should be up and about on a fair day like this.'

'Perchance they are sleeping off their midday meal,' suggested Gyrto. 'Or all but the babes and ancient crones are working in the fields.'

'Too late for that,' growled Conan. 'I like it not.'

'Or perchance they are in hiding, fearing robbery or murder.'

Conan said: 'Send two scouts through the village; we'll wait here.'

Two troopers hastened down the gentle slope and disappeared into the maw of the narrow, winding street. Soon the street disgorged them; and galloping towards their fellows, they signalled that all was quiet.

'Let's take a look ourselves,' growled Conan. And Gyrto waved his hundred lancers forward at a brisk trot.

The sun was a gigantic orange disc as it slipped to the western horizon; and the houses of Elymia stood black and sinister against its fiery glow. The rebels glanced about them with a touch of apprehension; for still there was no sign of human habitation in the squalid street or behind the shuttered doorways.

'Perhaps,' suggested Gyrto, 'the people heard of two approaching armies and fled, fearing to be caught betwixt hammer and anvil.'

Conan shrugged, loosening his sword in its scabbard. On each side of the roadway rose low cottages, their roofs thick-thatched. The front of one house was open, with a counter set before it. A painted mug above the humble door proclaimed it the village ale shop, the town being too small to boast an inn. Down the short street a barnlike building thrust itself back from the road. Scattered iron bars, a pincers and a brazier proved it a smithy; but no clang of metal issued from it. Something – he knew not what – raised the hairs on Conan's nape.

Conan twisted in the saddle to look back, as the last of his double column trotted into the deserted street. The pairs of horses pressed close against the walls of crowding houses, so meagre was the way.

'A mean place for an attack,' said Conan. 'Signal the men to hurry through.'

Gyrto waved an order to his trumpeter, when another

trumpet blared, close at hand. Instantly the doors of all the cottages burst open, and royalist soldiers boiled out, rending the dusk hideous with battle cries. They struck at Conan's troop from either side, their swords and pikes thirsty for blood.

Ahead three ranks of pikemen sprang into position, blocking the road with a wall of pointed steel. Slowly they moved forward, with battle lust in their eyes and spearheads glowing a dull crimson in the rays of the setting sun.

'Crom and Ishtar!' yelled Conan, sweeping out his sword, 'we're in Death's pocket! Gyrto, turn the men around!'

The din of battle rose – the shouts of angry men, the neighs of plunging steeds, the grind of steel on steel, the clash of swords on riven shields, and the dull thud of fallen bodies. Attacked from three sides by superior numbers, Conan's troopers were at a disadvantage. The confined space prevented them from bunching into a compact formation or working up speed for a charge. A lance in the hand of a charging horseman is more formidable than in the hand of that same horseman forced to halt.

The rebel troopers, spurred by fear and fury, set their lances and jabbed at their assailants. Some dropped their lances and, drawing swords, slashed downward at their attackers, raining well-aimed blows. Men swore loud oaths to their assorted gods. Injured horses reared and screamed like fiends in hell. One, disembowelled, fell kicking, pinning its rider; and the royalists swarmed upon the man, slashing and battering, until he lay incarnadined with gore.

Another rider, caught by an upflung spearhead, was lofted out of his saddle and tossed beneath the steel-shod hooves of a plunging steed. Still another was unhorsed, but he set his back to the wall of a house and stood off his attackers with the darting tongue of his sweeping blade.

Some of Count Ulric's soldiers went down beneath the rebels' lancepoints and swinging swords. Blood laid the dust on the earthern road, as wounded men shrieked in agony, the death rattle in their throats.

Roaring like a lion, Conan beat his way back along the

column, squeezing between his milling men and the enclosing walls. His great sword swung upward and descended; with nearly every blow, a royalist crumpled or fell dead. Thrice his down-directed cuts sheared arms from shoulders, and thrice blood spurted bubbling from the ghastly wounds. As Conan hewed, he shouted lustily.

'Out! Out! To the rear, march! Out of the village! Rally on the road!'

Powerful as was his voice, his words were drowned in a torrent of cacophony. But little by little his men wrenched their horses' heads around and pushed southward. Behind Conan, Captain Gyrto and two veteran lancers fought a desperate rear-guard action against the massed pikemen who pressed forward behind their bristling steel. Lances at the ready, they spurred their terror-stricken beasts against the wall of steel; but as one spearman fell, another leaped in to take his place. And so, despite their grim intent to win or die, they could not overwhelm the relentless surge of steel-clad men. And there one lancer died.

Conan's steed stumbled over a supine body. He jerked up on the bridle to prevent the animal's inadvertent fall. He swung a back-hand blow at a royalist swordsman, who caught the vicious stroke on his shield; but the sheer force of the blow hurled the soldier to his knees in a battered doorway, and kneeling, he cradled a broken arm, tears streaming down his face.

Finally, Conan glimpsed the last remnant of his troopers fighting free of their attackers and galloping up the slope beyond the scene of the débâcle. Between him and the retreating men, the narrow street was filled with royalists afoot, slipping on the bloodstained entrails of men and horses, swaying with fatigue, but like human bloodhounds, smelling out their prey, coming closer, ever closer to the three horsemen caught in the cruel jaws of the clever trap. Glancing to the right, Conan perceived between two cottages a narrow alley, a mere footpath among the weeds.

'Gyrto!' bellowed Conan. 'This way! Follow me!'

Abruptly turning his horse into that meagre alley, Conan paused only long enough to make sure the others followed closely. The lengthening shadows of a cottage enshrouded the fleeing men in darkness, and for a moment there was no yapping at their heels.

In the momentary respite, Conan reined in his exhausted mount and allowed the beast to pick its way among the crumpled vegetation. Suddenly, despite the gloaming, he descried a pigsty, its entrance barred by a battered panel, rope-bound to the adjacent fencing. With his bloodstained blade he severed the heavy rope, and the crude door swung open.

Gyrto and his companion stood aghast, wondering whether the heat of battle or a heavy blow had unseated their leader's reason. Then with an upraised finger pointing forward, Conan spurred his horse and, followed closely by his loyal troopers, sped down the narrow passageway.

A wave of racing royalist foot soldiers, interspersed with mounted men-at-arms, swirled round the corner of the cottage and crested in the slender channel of the alley.

Gyrto yelled to Conan: 'Ride man, ride! They're hot upon our trail.'

Conan bent low above his horse's neck, face buried in the creature's flowing mane. And then, at the alley's end, a tall fence, scarce visible in the gathering gloom, barred the way to safety.

Conan's horse, gathering its mighty haunches, rose magnificently and cleared the obstruction, with Gyrto's partner Sardus close upon its flying tail. But Gyrto was less lucky. His animal, too weary to take the jump, slammed into the barrier, and screamed with the agony of a broken neck.

Gyrto, thrown clear, leaped to his feet and drew his sword, prepared to sell his life dearly. Suddenly, the pursuing riders drew rein and swore at their rearing, dancing mounts, which in their panic pressed swordsmen against the cottage walls or struck them wicked blows from flailing hooves.

Gyrto marvelled at the hiatus in his almost sure destruction. 'Magic again?' he muttered between clenched teeth.

Then he spied the cause of his salvation. A sow and twenty piglets had ambled from their pen and, coated with evil-smelling muck, ran squealing through the weeds, rooting for edibles.

He heard Conan call: 'Climb the fence, man, quickly!' And, hesitating no longer, he flung himself at the rough barricade, dragged himself up, and scrambled over, just as the royalists reached the other side.

'Catch my stirrup!' roared Conan. 'Don't try to mount!'

Gyrto seized Conan's stirrup strap and bounded along with giant strides as the spurred beast gathered speed. At an easy canter they crossed the darkling fields, leaving the royalists behind.

When the village grew small in the distance, Conan pulled up. Peering about the fading landscape, he said, 'We shall catch up with the column presently. First I want a look at the enemy base. That hillock yonder may give a view of it.'

From the hilltop Conan stared across the intervening swells and hollows of the earth; and north of the village, he discovered a field encampment. It had been hidden from the village by a low rise; but seen from this height, its large expanse was evident. Scores of cooking fires twinkled in the twilight, and thin blue plumes of smoke wavered in the gentle breeze.

'There's Count Ulric's army,' said Conan. 'How many would you judge there be, Gyrto '

The captain thought the matter over. 'From the number of fires and the size of the camp, General, I should say a dozen regiments. What say you, Sardus?'

'At least twenty thousand men, sir,' said the veteran cavalryman. 'What standard's that, flapping atop a flagstaff over to the right?'

Conan squinted, forcing his catlike eyes to see despite the gathering dark. Then he exclaimed: 'Damn me for a Stygian, if that is not the standard of the Black Dragons!'

'Not the king's household guard, General?' exclaimed

Gyrto. 'That cannot be, unless Numedides himself is marching with Count Ulric.'

'I do not see the royal standard, so I doubt it,' rumbled Conan. 'Time we rejoined our comrades. It's a long road back to camp.'

Sardus mounted behind his footsore captain, and the trio began a cautious sweep around the village, wherein lay so many of their dead. Reaching the road at length, they hastened towards a stand of trees beneath which the survivors of the battle waited. At least a third of the sixty men were missing. Many wearing bandages helped to bind up their comrades' wounds.

As Conan, Gyrto and Sardus trotted up, the dispirited troopers raised a faint hurrah. Conan growled:

'I thank you all, but save your cheers for victory. I should have searched the houses ere leading you into a tyro's trap. Still, lads, you gave them better than you got. Now let's be on our way and hope to find our army camp by dawn.'

Next morning Conan told the tale of his adventures. Prospero whistled. 'Twenty thousand men! In a pitched battle they'd eat us alive.'

After swallowing a huge mouthful from a joint of beef, Conan said: 'Breathe not such thoughts, lest the prophecy invite its own fulfilment. Rout the men out – all save the scouts who fought at Elymia – and set them to fortifying the camp. With such numbers, Count Ulric might risk a night attack. Without ditch or stockade to detain him, he could crush us like insects beneath a wagon wheel.'

'But the Black Dragons!' cried Trocero. 'It is a thing incredible that Numedides should send his household troops to strengthen Ulric, leaving his person unprotected!'

Conan shrugged. 'I am sure of what I saw. No other unit carries for its symbol a winged monster on a field of black.'

Pallantides said: 'Sending the Black Dragons hither may leave Numedides vulnerable to attack, but it does naught to lessen our present problem.'

'If anything, their coming aggravates it,' added Trocero.

'Then be on your way, friends, and start the fortifications,' said Conan. 'We have no time to lose.'

A gentle morning breeze fanned a hastily erected palisade and cooled the bloodshot eyes and aching bodies of its builders. When the camp followers – sutlers, water boys, women and children – sought to carry water from a nearby stream, a company of royalist cavalry appeared over a rise, galloped down upon them, and sent them flying for their lives. One old man and one young child, slow to move, were slain.

A rebel scouting party was overtaken and forced to flee. When they regained the camp, their pursuers galloped past it, shouting taunts and hurling javelins into the stockade. Conan's archers, summoned hastily, brought down two of the enemy's horses, but comrades snatched their riders up and carried them away. Thus, although no real attack was launched against the rebels, Conan's weary men were worn down by tensions and alarums.

At the evening conference Publius said: 'While I am not a military man, General, I think we ought to slip away during the night, ere Ulric brings us down or starves us out. He has the force to do his will, since sickness, like a grey ghost, stalks amongst us.'

'I say,' said Trocero, banging the table with his fist, 'hold our position while my Poitanians raise the countryside. If Ulric surrounds us then, the countryfolk can throw a bigger ring around him.'

'With harvest time approaching,' Publius retorted, 'you'll find it difficult to raise a thousand. And farmers armed with naught but axe and pitchfork cannot withstand a charge of Ulric's armoured regulars. Would we were back in the Brocellian Forest, where our satyr friends could help us once again!'

Prospero put in: 'Aye, till the royalists learn to plug their ears – not longer. I say to launch a surprise attack this night on Ulric's camp.'

Pallantides shook his head. 'Naught more easily falls into confusion, with friend striking down friend, than a night attack with half-trained men like ours.'

The argument went round and round with no conclusion, while Conan sat sombrely, frowning but saying little. Then a sentry announced:

'A royalist officer and some fifty men have come in under a flag of truce, General. The officer asks to speak to you.'

'Disarm him and send him in,' said Conan, straightening in his chair.

The tent flap gaped, and in stalked a man in armour. The black heraldic eagle of Aquilonia was spread upon the breast of his white surcoat, while from his helmet rose the brazen wyvern of the Black Dragons. The officer saluted stiffly.

'General Conan? I am Captain Silvanus of the Black Dragons. I have come to join you with most of my troop, if you will have us.'

Conan looked the captain up and down through narrowed lids. He saw a tall, well-built, blond man, rather young for his captain's rating.

'Welcome, Captain Silvanus,' he said at last. 'I thank you for the offer. But before I accept it, I must know more of you.'

'Certainly, General. Do but ask.'

'First, what brings you to change sides at this juncture? You must know that our position is precarious, that Ulric outnumbers us, and that he is a competent commander. So wherefore turn your coat today?'

'It is simple, General Conan. My men and I have chosen a risk of death in the rebel cause over a safe life under that madman – if any life under the king's standard can be called safe.'

'But why at this particular time?'

'This is our first opportunity. The Dragons reached Elymia yestereve, before the skirmish twixt Ulric's men and yours. Had we set out from Tarantia to join you, forces loyal to the king would have barred our way and destroyed us.'

Conan asked: 'Has Numedides sent the whole of the Black Dragon regiment hither?'

'Aye, save for a few young lads in training.'

'Why does that dog denude himself of his personal guardians?'

'Numedides has proclaimed himself a god. He thinks himself immortal; and being invulnerable, has no need of bodyguards. Besides, he is determined to crush your rebellion and throws all contingents into Count Ulric's army. More march hither from the Eastern frontiers.'

'What of Thulandra Thuu, the king's magician?'

Silvanus's face grew pale. 'Demons are sometimes summoned by mention of their names, General Conan. During the madness of Numedides, the sorcerer rules the kingdom; and if less foolish than the king, he is as heartless and rapacious. His sacrifice of virgins for his unsavoury experiments is known to all.' Fumbling in his wallet, he brought out a miniature painted on alabaster and hung on a golden chain. The painting showed a girl of perhaps ten years of age.

'My daughter. She's dead,' said Silvanus. 'He took her. If the gods vouchsafe me a single chance, I will tear his throat out with my very teeth.' The captain's voice shook, and his hands trembled with the intensity of his emotion.

A savage gleam of blue balefire shone in Conan's eyes. His officers stirred uneasily, knowing that mistreatment of women roused the ruthless Cimmerian's furious indignation. He showed the miniature around and returned it to Silvanus, saying:

'We want more information on Count Ulric's army. How many are they?'

'Nearly twenty-five thousand, I believe.'

'Whence did Ulric get so many? The Army of the North had no such strength when I left the mad king's service.'

'Many of Prince Numitor's Frontiersmen, when they recovered from their panic, rallied and joined Count Ulric. And the regiment of the Black Dragons was ordered from Tarantia.'

'What befell Numitor after the rout?'

'He slew himself in despair over his failure.'

'Are you certain?' asked Conan. 'Amulius Procas was said to have killed himself, but I know that he was murdered.'

'There is no doubt of it, sir. Prince Numitor stabbed himself before witnesses.'

'A pity,' said Trocero. 'He was the most decent of the lot, if too simple-hearted for a bloody civil war.'

Conan rumbled: 'This calls for discussion. Pallantides, find sleeping quarters for Captain Silvanus and his men; then rejoin us here. Good night, Captain.'

Publius, who had said little, now spoke up: 'A moment, if you please, Captain Silvanus. Who was your father?'

The officer, at the tent flap, turned. 'Silvius Macro, sir. Why do you ask?'

'I knew him when I served the king as treasurer. Good night.'

When the captain had departed, Conan said: 'Well, what think you? At least, it's good to have men deserting to us – not from us – for a change.'

'I think,' said Prospero, 'that Thulandra Thuu seeks to plant a new assassin in our midst. He'll but await the chance to slide a knife between your ribs, then ride like a fiend from hell.'

Trocero said: 'I disagree. He looked to me like a straightforward young officer, not like one of Numedides's fellow-debauchees or Thulandra's ensorcelled minions.'

'You cannot trust appearances,' rejoined Prospero. 'An apple may look never so rosy and still be filled with worms.'

'If you will permit me,' interrupted Publius, 'I knew the young man's father. He was a fine, upstanding citizen – and still is, if he lives.'

'Like father not always is like son,' grumbled Prospero.

'Prospero,' said Conan, 'your concern for my safety does me honour. But a man must take his chances, especially in war. However much you guard me against a secret dagger,

Ulric is like to kill us one and all, unless by some sudden stroke we can reverse our fortunes.'

For an instant there was silence as Conan sat brooding, his deep-set blue eyes focused on the ground before him. At last he said:

'I have a plan – a perilous plan, yet fraught with no more danger than our present situation. Tarantia is defenceless, stripped of her soldiery, whilst mad Numedides plays immortal god upon his throne. A band of desperate men, disguised as Dragons of the Household Guard, might reach the palace and –'

'Conan!' shouted Trocero. 'An inspiration from the gods! I'll lead the foray.'

'You are too important to Poitain, my lord,' said Prospero. 'It is I who –'

'Neither of you goes,' said Conan firmly. 'Poitanians are not greatly loved in the central provinces, whose people have not forgotten your invasion of their land during the war with King Vilerus.'

'Who then?' asked Trocero. 'Pallantides?'

Conan shook his full black mane, and his face glowed with the lust of battle. 'I shall perform this task as best I may, or die in the trying. I'll choose a squad of seasoned veterans, and we'll borrow surcoats and helmets from Captain Silvanus's men. Silvanus – I'll bring him, also, to identify us at the gates. Aye, he is the key to the city.'

Publius held up a cautionary hand. 'A moment, gentlemen. Conan's plan might well succeed in ordinary warfare. But in Tarantia you deal not merely with a demented king but also with a malevolent sorcerer, whose mystic passes and words of magic can move mountains and call demons from the earth or sea or sky.'

'Wizards don't terrify me,' said Conan. 'Years ago, in Khoraja, I faced one of the deadliest and slew him despite his flutterings and mutterings.'

'How did you that?' asked Trocero.

'I threw my sword at him.'

'Do not count on such a feat again,' said Publius. 'Your strength is great and your senses keener than those of common men; but fortune is not always kind, even to heroes.'

'When my time comes, it comes,' growled Conan.

'But your time may well be our time, too,' said Prospero. 'Let me send for Dexitheus. A Mitrian priest knows more of the world beyond than we ordinary mortals do.'

Conan gave in, albeit with ill grace.

Dexitheus listened with folded hands to Conan's plan. At length he spoke gravely: 'Publius is right, Conan. Do not underestimate the power of Thulandra Thuu. We of the priesthood have some notion of the dark, nameless forces beyond man's fathoming.'

'Whence comes this pestilent thaumaturge?' asked Trocero. 'Men say he is a Vendhyan; others, a Stygian.'

'Neither,' replied Dexitheus. 'In my priestly brotherhood we call him a Lemurian, coming – I know not how – from islands far beyond the known world, eastward, in the ocean beyond Khitai. These shrouded isles are all that remains of a once spacious land that sank beneath the waves. To outwit a sorcerer with powers such as his, our general needs more than material arms and armour.'

Trocero asked: 'Are there no wizards in this camp who would accept this service?'

'Nay!' snorted Conan. 'I have no use for tricksters such as those. I would not harbour one or seek his aid.'

Dexitheus's expression became doleful. 'General, though you know it not, I am much discomfited.'

'How so, Reverence?' said Conan. 'I owe you much and would not distress you without cause. Speak not in riddles, good friend.'

'You have no use for wizards, General, calling them charlatans and quacks; yet there is one you count among your friends. You have need of a magician; yet you refuse the help of such a one.' Dexitheus paused and Conan beckoned him to continue.

'Know, then, that in my youth I studied the black arts,

albeit I advanced little beyond the lowest grades of sorcery. Later I saw the light of Mitra and forswore all dealings with demons and the forces of the occult. Had the priesthood learned of my wizardly past, I should not have been admitted to their order. Therefore, when I accompany you on this perilous mission –'

'What, you?' cried Conan, frowning. 'Wizard or no, you are too old to gallop a hundred leagues! You would not survive it.'

'On the contrary, I am of tougher fibre than you think. The ascetic life lends me a vigour far beyond my years, and you will need me to cast a counter-spell or two. But when I accompany you, my secret will come out. I shall be forced to resign my holy office – a sad ending to my life's career.'

'Meseems the use of magic for a worthy end is a forgivable sin,' said Conan.

'To you, sir; not to my order, which is most intolerant in the matter. But I have no alternative; I shall use what powers I have for Aquilonia.' His sigh was heavy with tears too deep for thought.

'After it's over,' said Conan, 'perchance I can persuade your priesthood to make exception to the rigour of their rules. Prepare, good friend, to leave within the hour.'

'This very night?'

'When better? If we wait upon the morrow, we may find the camp hemmed in by royalists. Prospero, pick me a troop of your most skilful mounted fighters. See that each man has not one horse, but two, to allow for frequent changes. But do it quietly. We must outrun the news of our departure. As for the rest of you, keep the men busy improving our defences whilst I am gone. To all of you, farewell!'

The half-moon barely cleared the treetops when a column of horsemen, each leading a spare mount, issued stealthily from the rebel camp. In the lead rode Conan, wearing the helmet and white surcoat of the Black Dragons. With him rode Captain Silvanus, and behind them trotted Dexitheus, priest of Mitra, likewise attired. Fifty of Conan's most trusted troopers followed, disguised in the same manner as their leaders.

Under Silvanus's guidance, the column swung wide of the royalist encampment. When they were once again on the Tarantia road, they broke into a steady trot. The moon set, and black night swallowed up the line of desperate men.

XII

Darkness in the Moonlight

The sun had set, and overhead a brilliant half-moon hung
suspended in a cloudless sky. At the royal palace of Tarantia,
the king's solitary supper, served on gold platters in his
private dining-room, had been cleared away. Save for a taster
standing behind the royal armchair, two bodyguards stationed
at the silver-studded doorway, and the footmen who served
the royal meats, none had attended him to join in the repast.

Thousands of lamps and candles blazed in the royal
chambers—so bountiful the light that a stranger, entering,
would wonder whether a coronation or a neighbouring
monarch's visit occasioned this opulent display.

Yet the palace seemed curiously deserted. Instead of the
chatter of lovely ladies, chivalrous youths and high-ranking
nobles of the kingdom, echoes from the past reverberated
down the marble halls, empty save for a few guards, on whose
silvered breastplates the multitude of candles were reflected.
The guards were either adolescent boys or greybeard oldsters;
for when the household guard marched south to confront the
rebels, the king's officials had hastily replaced the corps of
the Black Dragons with lads in training and retired veterans.

The lamps and candles burned all night, as the king—
fancying himself a sun god—deemed naught but the light
of day at night worthy of his exalted station. Thus, scurrying
servants hastened from lamp to lamp to assure sufficient oil
in each and carried armfuls of candles from chandelier to
chandelier to replace those that flickered out.

As the king's madness waxed, the courtiers and civil servants, normally in attendance, stole away. Foremost among
these was Vibius Latro, who had offices and living quarters
in the palace. The chancellor had sent a message to Nume-

dides, begging a short leave of absence. His health, the note continued, was breaking down from long hours of work, and without a brief respite at his country seat, he feared he could no longer further the interests of His Majesty.

Having just flogged one of his concubines to death, Numedides, in rare good humour, granted his request. Latro forthwith loaded his family into a travelling carriage and set out for his estates, north of Tarantia. At the first crossroads, he veered eastward and, lashing his horses, raced for the Nemedian border two hundred leagues away. Other members of the king's official family likewise found compelling reasons for a leave of absence and speedily departed.

Numedides's throne in the Chamber of Private Audience stood upon a patterned Iranistani carpet, woven of fine wools artfully dyed to the colour of rubies, jades, amethysts and sapphires and shot through with threads of gold. The chair itself, an ornate structure, though less imposing than the Ruby Throne in the Public Throne Room, was tastelessly embellished with dragons, lions, swords and stars. The heraldic eagle of the Numedidean dynasty soared up from the tall back, its wings and eyes studded with precious stones that sparkled in the generous candlelight.

The king's silver sceptre – the ceremonial symbol of kingship – lay across the purple-pillowed seat, while the Sword of State, a great two-handed weapon, bejewelled of hilt and scabbard, reposed on one of the chair's broad arms.

Two persons stood in the chamber: King Numedides, wearing the slender golden circlet that was the crown of Aquilonia and a crimson robe bespotted with stains of food, wine and vomit; and Alcina, clad in a clinging gown of sea-green silk.

From opposite sides of the gilt throne they glared at each other. Alcina hissed:

'You mangy old dog! I will die before I submit to your perversions! You cannot catch me, you old, fat, filthy heap of offal! Go find a bitch or a sow to vent your lusts upon! Like to like!'

'I said I would not hurt you, little spitfire!' wheezed Numedides. 'But catch you I will! None can escape the desires of a king, let alone a god! Come here!'

Numedides suddenly moved sidewise, in a feint at which he showed himself surprisingly nimble. Caught unawares, Alcina leaped back, losing the protection of the ornate chair. Then, with outspread arms and clutching hands, the king herded her into a corner far removed from either pair of double doors, whose pilastered frames adorned the walls to left and right of the ostentatious throne.

Alcina's fingers flew to her bodice and whipped out a slender dagger, tipped with the same poison that had slain Amulius Procas. 'Keep back, I warn you!' she cried. 'One prick of this, and you will die!'

Numedides gave back a step. 'You little fool, know you not that I am impervious to your envenomed bodkin?'

'We shall soon see whether you are or not, if you approach me closer.'

The king retreated to his throne and caught up his sceptre. Then once more he stalked the trembling girl. When Alcina raised her dagger, he struck a blow with his silver club, hitting her hand. The dagger spun away and bounced across the carpet, while Alcina, with a cry of anguish, caught her bruised hand to her breast.

'Now, you little witch,' said Numedides, 'we shall —'

The pair of doors on the right side of the audience chamber sprang open. Thulandra Thuu, leaning on his carven staff, stood on the threshold.

'How came you here?' thundered Numedides. 'The doors were locked!'

The dark-skinned sorcerer's sibilant voice was the crack of a whip. 'Your Majesty! I warned you not to molest my servants!'

The king scowled. 'We were just playing a harmless game. And who are you to warn a god of aught? Who is the ruler here?'

Thulandra Thuu smiled a thin and bitter smile. 'You reign

here, but you do not rule. I do.'

Numedides's jowls empurpled with his waxing wrath. 'You blasphemous ghoul! Out of my sight, ere I blast you with my lightnings!'

'Calm yourself, Majesty. I have news—'

The king's voice rose to a scream: 'I said *get out*! I'll show you—'

Numedides's groping hand brushed the hilt of the Sword of State. He drew the ponderous blade from its jewelled scabbard and advanced upon Thulandra Thuu, swinging the weapon with both hands. The sorcerer calmly awaited his approach.

With an incoherent shriek, the king whirled the sword in a decapitating blow. At the last instant Thulandra, whose expression had not changed, brought up his staff to parry. Steel and carven wood met with a ringing crash, as if Thulandra, too, wielded a massive sword. With a dexterous twirl of his staff, the sorcerer whipped the weapon from the king's hands and sent it flying upwards, turning over and over in the air. As it descended, the blade struck Numedides in the face, laying open a finger-long gash in the king's cheek. Blood trickled into his rusty beard.

Numedides clapped a hand to his cheek and stared stupidly at the blood dripping from his fingers. 'I bleed, just like a mortal!' he mumbled. 'How can that be?'

'You have a distance yet to go ere you wear the mantle of divinity,' said Thulandra Thuu with a narrow smile.

The king bellowed in a sudden rage of fear: 'Slaves! Pages! Phaedo! Manius! Where in the nine hells are you? Your divine master is being murdered!'

'It will do him no good,' said Alcina, evenly. 'He told me that he had ordered all his servants elsewhere in the palace, so I might scream my head off to no avail.' And she tossed back her night-tipped hair with her uninjured hand.

'Where are my loyal subjects?' whimpered Numedides. 'Valerius! Procas! Thespius! Gromel! Volmana! Where are my courtiers? Where is Vibius Latro? Has everyone deserted me? Does no one love me any more, despite all I have done for Aquilonia?' The abandoned monarch began to weep.

'As you know in your more lucid moments,' the sorcerer said sternly, 'Procas is dead; Vibius Latro has fled; and Gromel has deserted to the enemy. Volmana is fighting under Count Ulric, as are the others. Now, pray sit down and listen; I have things of moment to relate.'

Waddling to the throne, Numedides sank down, his spotted robe billowing about him. He pulled a dirty kerchief from his sleeve and pressed it to his wounded cheek, where it grew red with blood.

'Unless you can better control yourself,' said Thulandra Thuu, 'I shall have to do away with you and rule directly, instead of through you as before.'

'You never will be king!' mumbled Numedides. 'Not a man in Aquilonia would obey you. You are not of royal blood. You are not an Aquilonian. You are not even a Hyborian. I begin to doubt if you are even a human being.' He paused, glowering. 'So even if we hate each other, you need me as much as I need you.

'Well, what is this news at which you hint? Good news, I hope. Speak up, sir sorcerer; do not keep me in suspense!'

'If you will but listen . . . I cast our horoscopes this afternoon and discovered the imminence of deadly peril.'

'Peril? From what source?'

'That I cannot say; the indications were unclear. It surely cannot be the rebel army. My visions on the astral plane, confirmed by yesterday's message from Count Ulric, inform me that the rebels are penned beyond Elymia. They will soon retreat in the face of hopeless odds, disperse in despair, or suffer annihilation. We have naught to fear from them.'

'Could that devil Conan have slipped past Count Ulric?'

'Alas, my astral visions are not clear enough to distinguish individuals from afar. But the barbarian is a resourceful rascal; when you drove him into flight, I warned you might not have seen the last of him.'

'I have had reports of bands of traitors within sight of

the city walls,' said the king, lips quivering in petulant uncertainty.

'That is gossip and not truth, unless some new leader has arisen among the disaffected of the Central Provinces.'

'Suppose such scum does wash ashore and lap the city walls? What can we do with the Black Dragons far away? It was your idea to have them join Count Ulric.' The king's voice grew shrill, as fear and rage snapped the thin thread of his composure. He ranted on:

'I left the management of this campaign to you, because you claim a store of arcane wisdom. Now I see that in military matters you are the merest tyro. You have bungled everything! When you sent Procas into Argos, you said that this incursion would snuff out the rebel menace, once and for all; but it did not. You assured me that the rabble would never cross the Alimane, and lo! the Border Legion was broken and dispersed. Quoth you, they had no chance of passing the Imirian Escarpment, and yet the rebels did. Finally, the plague you sent among them, you said, would surely wipe the upstarts out, and yet —'

'Your Majesty!' A young voice severed the king's recriminations. 'Pray, let me in! It is a dire emergency!'

'That is one of my pages; I know his voice,' said Numedides, rising and going to the still-locked door on the left side of the throne. When he had turned the key, a youth in page's garb burst in, gasping: 'My lord! The rebel Conan has seized the palace!'

'Conan!' cried the king. 'What has befallen? Speak!'

'A troop of the Black Dragons – or men apparelled in their garb – galloped up to the palace gates, crying that they had urgent messages from the front. The guards thought nothing of it and passed them through, but I recognised the huge Cimmerian when I saw his scarred face in the lighted ante-room. I knew him in the Westermarck, ere I came to Tarantia to serve Your Majesty. And so I ran to warn you.'

'Mean you he is about to burst upon us, with no guards in the palace save a scrawny pack of striplings and their grandsires?' Eyes ablaze with fury, he turned to Thulandra Thuu. 'Well, you sorcerous scoundrel, work a deterrent spell!'

The magician was already making passes with his staff and speaking in a sibilant, unknown tongue. As the sonorous sentences rolled out, a strange phenomenon occurred. The candles dimmed, as if the room were filled with swirling smoke or roiling fogs from evening marshes, dank with decay. Darker and darker grew the atmosphere, until the Chamber of Private Audience became as black as a dungeon rock-sealed for centuries.

The king cried out in terror: 'Have you blinded me?'

'Quiet, Majesty! I have cast a spell of darkness over the palace, a magical defence. If we do lock the doors and speak in whispers, the invaders will not discover us.'

The page felt his way across the wide expanse of carpet and turned the great key in the left pair of doors, while Alcina, lithe as a jaguar, likewise barred the right-hand portal. The king retreated to his throne and sat in silence, too terrified to speak. Alcina sought the slender body of the sorcerer and huddled at his feet in mute supplication. The page, uncertain of his whereabouts, shrank back from the door whose key he turned and wished himself home in the humble alleys of Tarantia. The silence was complete, save for the beating of four frightened hearts.

Suddenly the page's door sprang open, and a chant could be heard in the ancient Hyborian tongue. The blackness thinned and rolled away, and the light of many candles once more flooded the utmost corners of the audience chamber.

In the open doorway stood Conan the Cimmerian, bloody sword in hand; and at his side Dexitheus, the priest of Mitra, still crooned the final phrases of his potent incantation.

'Slay them, Thulandra,' shrieked Numedides, eyes starting at the sight of his former general. He held the bloody kerchief to his injured cheek and moaned. Alcina shrank closer to her mentor and stared with baleful eyes upon the man who had survived her deadly potion.

Thulandra Thuu raised his carven staff, thrust it at Conan, and, in the language of his undiscoverable bourn, spat out a curse or else a ringing invocation to an unknown god. A rippling flash of light, like a blue streak of living fire, sped from the staff tip towards the Cimmerian's armoured breast. With the dread rattling of a thunderclap, the bolt shattered against an unseen barrier, spattering sparks.

Frowning, Thulandra Thuu repeated his cantrip, louder and in a voice of deep authority, shifting his aim to Dexitheus. Again the blue flame zigzagged across the intervening space and spread out, like water tossed against a pane of glass.

As Conan started for the sorcerer, his blue eyes blazing with the lust to kill, Captain Silvanus jostled past him, shouting:

'You who slew my daughter! I seek revenge!'

Silvanus, with madness glinting in his bloodshot eyes, rushed at the sorcerer, sword raised above his head. But before he had gone three paces, the magician pointed his staff and once again cried out. Again the blue lightning illumined the room with its awful radiance; and Silvanus, uttering a scream of horror, pitched forward on his face.

A hole the thickness of a man's thumb opened on the back plate of his cuirass, and the blackened steel curled into the petals of a rose of death. A red stain slowly spread over the Iranistani carpet and mingled with the jewelled tones of its weaving.

Conan wasted no time lamenting his companion but strode briskly towards the sorcerer, his sword upraised to strike. The page, ashen-pale, scuttled behind the throne; Alcina and the king flattened themselves against opposing walls.

But Thulandra Thuu had not exhausted his resources. He gripped the two ends of his staff in his bony hands and held it at arm's length in front of him, chanting the while in a tongue that was old when the seas swallowed Lemuria. As Conan took another step, he encountered a strange resistance that brought him to a halt.

Elastic and yielding was this invisible surface; yet it confounded Conan's most strenuous attack. The cords in his massive neck stood out; his face darkened with his almost superhuman effort; his muscles writhed like pythons. Yet the formless barrier held. As he thrust his sword into that invisible substance, he saw Thulandra's staff bend in the middle, as if impelled by an opposing force, but it did not break. Dexitheus's mightiest magic had no power against the staff and the protection it afforded to Thulandra Thuu.

At last the sorcerer spoke, and his voice was weary with the weight of many years. 'I see yon renegade priest of Mitra has armoured you against my bolts; but for all his puny magic, he cannot destroy me. Aquilonia is unworthy of my efforts. I shall remove to a land beyond the sunrise, where people will value my experiments and the gift of life eternal. Farewell!'

'Master! Master! Take me with you!' cried Alcina, raising her arms in humble supplication.

'Nay, girl, stay back! I have no further use for you.'

Thulandra Thuu edged to the door by which he had entered the audience chamber. As he moved, the elastic barrier he maintained retreated also. Lips bared in a mirthless grin, blue eyes ablaze, Conan followed the lean sorcerer step by step. His magnificent body quivered with the controlled fury of a lion deprived of its prey.

As they reached the doorway whence the sorcerer had entered, Thulandra Thuu began to sway, then to revolve. He spun faster and faster, until his dark figure became a blur. Suddenly he vanished.

As the wizard disappeared, the unseen barrier faded. Conan sprang forward, his sword upraised for a murderous slash. With a blistering curse, he rushed into the corridor. But the hall was empty. He listened, but he could detect no footfall.

Shaking his tousled mane as if to put a dream to flight, Conan turned back to the Chamber of Private Audience. He found Dexitheus guarding the other door, Alcina pressed against the farther wall, and King Numedides seated on his throne, dabbing his injured face with his bloody kerchief. Conan strode quickly to the throne to confront the king.

'Stand, mortal!' bawled Numedides, pointing a pudgy

forefinger. 'Know that I am a god! I am King of Aquilonia!'

Conan shot out an arm in which the hard muscles writhed like serpents. Seizing the king's robe, he hauled the madman to his feet. 'You mean,' he snarled, 'you were king. Have you aught to say before you die?'

Numedides wilted, a pool of molten tallow in a burned-out candle. Tears coursed down his flabby face to mingle with the blood that still oozed from his wound. He sank to his knees, babbling:

'Pray, do not slay me, gallant Conan! Though I have committed errors, I intended only well for Aquilonia! Send me into exile, and I shall not return. You cannot kill an ageing, unarmed man!'

With a contemptuous snort, Conan hurled Numedides to the floor. He wiped his sword on the hem of the fallen monarch's garment and sheathed it. Turning on his heel, he said:

'I do not hunt mice. Tie up this scum until we find a madhouse to confine him.'

A sudden flicker of movement seen beyond the corner of his eye and sharp intake of breath by Dexitheus warned Conan of impending danger. Numedides had found the poisoned dagger dropped by Alcina and now, weapon in hand, he rose to make one last, desperate lunge to stab the Liberator in the back.

Conan wheeled, shot out his left hand and caught the descending wrist. His right hand seized Numedides's flaccid throat and, straining the mighty muscles in his arm, Conan forced his attacker down upon the throne. With his free hand the king wrenched in vain at Conan's obdurate wrist. His legs thrashed spasmodically.

As Conan's iron fingers dug deeper into the pudgy neck, Numedides's eyes bulged. His mouth gaped, but no sound issued forth. Deeper and deeper sank Conan's python grip, until the others in the room, standing with suspended breath, heard the cartilage crack. Blood trickled from the corner of the king's mouth, to mingle with the sanguine rheum that had besmeared his face and beard and hair.

Numedides's face turned blue, and little by little his flailing arms went limp. The poisoned dagger thudded to the floor and spun into a corner. Conan maintained his crushing grip until all life had fled.

At last Conan released the corpse, which tumbled off the throne in a dishevelled heap. The Cimmerian drew a long breath, then spun around and whipped his blade from its scabbard, as running feet and rattling armour clattered down the hall. A score of his men, who had been wandering around the palace in search of him, crowded into the doorway to the chamber. All voices stilled, all eyes were turned upon him, as he stood, legs spread and sword in hand, beside the throne of Aquilonia, a look of triumph in his blazing eyes.

What thoughts raced through Conan's mind at that moment, none ever knew. But finally he sheathed his sword, bent down, and tore the bloody crown from the bedraggled head of dead Numedides. Holding the slender circlet in one hand, he unbuckled the chin strap of his helmet with the other and tugged the headpiece off. Then he raised the crown in both his hands and placed it on his head.

'Well,' he said, 'how does it look?'

Dexitheus spoke up: 'Hail, King Conan of Aquilonia!'

The others took up the cry; and at last even the page, who stared owl-eyed from his hiding place behind the throne, joined in.

Alcina, moving forward with the seductive dancer's grace that had so excited Conan in Messantia, glided in front of him and fell prettily to her knees.

'Oh, Conan!' she cried, 'it was ever you I loved. But alas, I was ensorcelled and forced to do the bidding of that wicked thaumaturge. Forgive me and I will be your faithful servant forevermore!'

Frowning, Conan looked down upon her, and his voice was thunder rumbling in the hills. 'When someone has sought to murder me, I'd be a fool to give that one a second chance. Were you a man, I'd slay you here and now. But I do not war on women, so begone.

'If after this night you are found within those parts that

have declared for me, you'll lose your pretty head. Elatus, accompany her to the stables, saddle her a horse, and see her to the outskirts of Tarantia.'

Alcina went, the black cloud of her silken hair hiding her countenance. At the door she turned back to look once more at Conan, tears glistening on her cheeks. Then she was gone.

Conan kicked the corpse of Numedides. 'Stick this carrion's head on a spear and display it in the city, then carry it to Count Ulric in Elymia, to convince him and his army that a new king rules in Aquilonia.'

One of Conan's troopers shouldered his way into the crowded room. 'General Conan!'

'Well?'

The man paused to catch his breath. His eyes were big as buttons. 'You ordered Cadmus and me to guard the palace gates. Well, just now we heard a horse and chariot coming from the stables, but neither beast nor carriage did we see. Then Cadmus pointed to the ground, and there was a shadow on the moonlit road, like to a horse and cart. It ran along the ground, but naught there was to cast the shadow!'

'What did you?'

'Did, sir? What could we do? The shadow passed through the open gates and vanished down the street. So I came arunning to tell you.'

'The late king's sorcerer and his man, I doubt not,' said Conan to his assembled company. 'Let them go; the he-witch said he would betake himself to some distant eastern bourn. He'll trouble us no more.' Then turning to Dexitheus, he said: 'We must set up a government on the morrow, and you shall be my chancellor.'

The priest cried out in great distress. 'Oh, no, Gen – Your Majesty! I must take up a hermit's life, to atone for my resort to magic despite the regulations of my order.'

'When Publius joins us, you may do so with my blessing. In the interim we need a government, and you are wise in matters politic. Round up the officials and their clerks by noon.'

Dexitheus sighed. 'Very well, my lord King.' He looked

down on Silvanus's body and sadly shook his head. 'I much regret the death of this young man, but I could not maintain defensive fields around you both.'

'He died a soldier's death; we'll bury him with honours,' Conan said. 'Where can one take a bath in this marble barn?'

Newly shaven and shorn, his mighty frame arrayed in ebon velvet, Conan rested on the purple-pillowed throne in the Chamber of Private Audience. All traces of violence had been erased – the bodies removed, the poisoned dagger buried, the carpet scrubbed free of bloodstains. An expectant smile lit Conan's craggy countenance.

Then Chancellor Publius bustled in with several scrolls under his velvet-coated arm. 'My lord,' he began, 'I have here – '

'Crom's devils!' Conan burst out. 'Cannot that business wait? Prospero is bringing in a score of beauties who have volunteered to be the king's companions. I am to choose among them.'

'Sire!' said Publius sternly. 'Some of these matters require immediate attention. 'Twill not hurt the young women to wait a while.

'Here, for example, is a petition from the barony of Castria, begging to be forgiven their arrears in taxes. Here are the treasury accounts. And here the advocates' briefs in the lawsuit of Phinteas versus Arius Priscus, which is being appealed before the throne. The suit has continued undecided for sixteen years.

'Here is a letter from one Quesado of Kordava, a former spy of Vibius Latro. Meseems that we had dealings with him before.'

'What does that dog want?' snorted Conan.

'He begs employment in his former capacity, as intelligence agent to His Majesty.'

'Aye, he was good at skulking around and acting like a winesop or an idiot. Give him a post – on trial, but never send him as an envoy to a fellow monarch.'

'Yes, Sire. Here is the petition for pardon for Galenus

Selo. And here is another petition, this one from the copper-smiths' guild. They want –'

'Gods and devils!' shouted Conan, slamming a hairy fist into his other hand. 'Why did no one tell me that kingship entails this dreary drudgery? I'd almost rather be a pirate on the main!'

Publius smiled. 'Even the lightest crown sits heavily be-times. A ruler has to rule, or another will govern in his stead. The late Numedides shirked his proper tasks, and he was –'

Conan sighed. 'Yes, yes. I suppose you're right, Crom curse it. Page! Fetch a table and spread out these documents. Now, Publius, the treasury statements first . . .'

CONAN

☐ 11452-0	**CONAN, #1**	$2.95
☐ 11453-9	**CONAN OF CIMMERIA, #2**	$2.95
☐ 11863-1	**CONAN THE FREEBOOTER, #3**	$2.95
☐ 11597-7	**CONAN THE WANDERER, #4**	$2.95
☐ 11858-5	**CONAN THE ADVENTURER, #5**	$2.95
☐ 11585-3	**CONAN THE BUCCANEER, #6**	$2.95
☐ 11586-1	**CONAN THE WARRIOR, #7**	$2.95
☐ 11589-6	**CONAN THE USURPER, #8**	$2.95
☐ 11590-X	**CONAN THE CONQUEROR, #9**	$2.95
☐ 11471-7	**CONAN THE AVENGER, #10**	$2.95
☐ 11472-5	**CONAN OF AQUILONIA, #11**	$2.95
☐ 11623-X	**CONAN OF THE ISLES, #12**	$2.95
☐ 11716-3	**CONAN: THE FLAME KNIFE**	$2.95
☐ 11628-0	**CONAN THE MERCENARY**	$2.95
☐ 11479-2	**CONAN THE SWORDSMAN**	$2.95